CRAZY DIAMOND

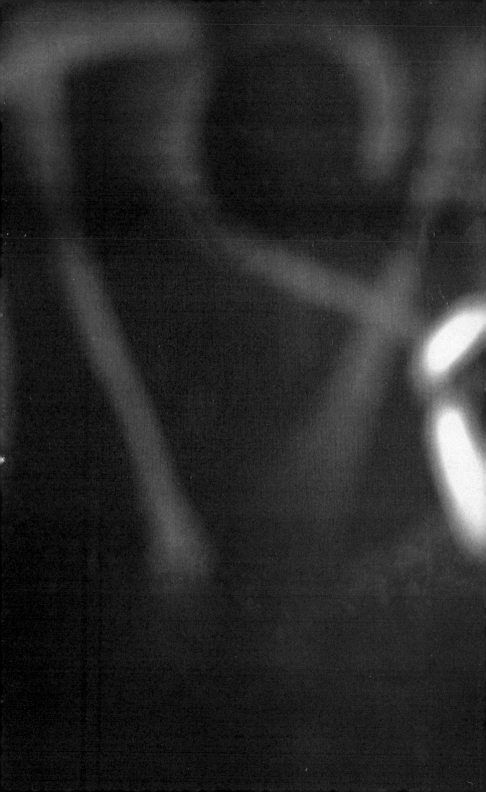

CRAZY

Also by David Chotjewitz

Daniel Half Human

CRAZY
DIAMOND

DAVID CHOTJEWITZ

TRANSLATED BY DORIS ORGEL

A RICHARD JACKSON BOOK
ATHENEUM BOOKS FOR YOUNG READERS
NEW YORK LONDON TORONTO SYDNEY

Atheneum Books for Young Readers
An imprint of Simon & Schuster Children's Publishing Division
1230 Avenue of the Americas, New York, New York 10020
This book is a work of fiction. Any references to historical events, real people, or
real locales are used fictitiously. Other names, characters, places, and incidents are
products of the author's imagination, and any resemblance to actual events or locales
or persons, living or dead, is entirely coincidental.
Book design by Michael McCartney
The text for this book is set in Serifa and Gill Sans.
Manufactured in the United States of America
10 9 8 7 6 5 4 3 2 1
Library of Congress Cataloging-in-Publication Data
Chotjewitz, David.
Crazy diamond / David Chotjewitz ; translated by Doris Orgel. —1st ed.
p.   cm.
"A Richard Jackson Book."
Summary: Chronicles the meteoric rise and fall of a young pop music star in Germany,
as well as the relationships she builds and destroys along the way.
ISBN-13: 978-1-4169-1176-0
ISBN-10: 1-4169-1176-6
[1. Fame—Fiction. 2. Interpersonal relations—Fiction. 3. Musicians—Fiction.
4. Popular music—Fiction. 5. Death—Fiction. 6. Music trade—Fiction.
7. Hamburg (Germany)—Fiction. 8. Germany—Fiction.] I. Orgel, Doris. II. Title.
PZ7.C4463548Cra 2008
[Fic]—dc22
2006030287

The author and publisher wish to acknowledge the following for permission to
reprint the copyrighted material listed below. Every effort has been made to locate all
persons having any rights or interests in the material published here. Any existing
rights not here acknowledged will, if the author or publisher is notified, be duly
acknowledged in future editions of this book:

The song "Not in a Thousand Years" © by Jana Behnke.
The passage "Today you will become a stranger to me" on p. 139 goes back to a text
by Jara Jovanović.

WE ALL LEAD TWO LIVES,
ONE THAT WE DREAM,
AND ANOTHER THAT
BRINGS US TO THE GRAVE.
————————FERNANDO PESSOA

REMEMBER WHEN YOU
WERE YOUNG
YOU SHONE LIKE THE SUN
SHINE ON YOU CRAZY
DIAMOND!
————————————PINK FLOYD

CONTENTS

CD 1: CRAZY DIAMOND

CD 2: THE RISE AND FALL OF MIRA M.

CD 1: CRAZY DIAMOND

[INTRO]
MIRA REMIXED

1. The sturgeons swam on top, as always, scavenging for food, their mouths moving up and down the glass walls like vacuum cleaners. And the eel, who usually slept by day, slithered among the water plants. Lighting tubes and algae made the water bright green, but now it was tinged faintly red.

The aquarium was almost six feet long. Mira fit in easily. Her hair floated upward on bubbles of air. Wisps of blood seeped from tiny holes the eel had bitten in her body. She lay facedown, as though searching for something that had sunk to the bottom.

Rosa was one of those people who always look chic, even now, wearing a jogging suit and a bulky down coat. She had gleaming black skin and big, luminous eyes—like an African princess, OK said often—a princess with an edge to her, and a scathing wit.

Just now she looked solemn, eyes cast down, trying to avoid the puddles around the aquarium.

She stopped a short distance from it and gazed at the pale body—Mira in the white T-shirt, black hair floating like sea grass. Cautiously she drew nearer, placed one hand on Mira's back, pulled her to the glass wall, turned her over, and, using both arms, strained to lift her over the rim of the tank.

Mira wasn't heavy, a hundred pounds at most, although her body had already begun to bloat. Rosa noticed the narrow wound on Mira's forehead. She put her ear close to Mira's mouth. Mira did not breathe. Her lips were as cold as the water.

For a moment Rosa's brain refused to take it in. Just last night, a few hours ago, Mira had sat next to her on the couch, exhausted, pale, trembling. But alive.

This mouth, which now no longer breathed, had opened, closed, said things. And these eyes, now staring into emptiness, had looked around—although slowly, and with dilated pupils.

Mindless of the puddles, Rosa hurried to the phone. She thought for a moment, then chose OK's number. When she didn't reach him at the office, she tried his cell. No answer there, either. She sat down at the large table and looked from the phone to the aquarium, then to the giant window from which you could see the Elbe and the harbor.

She took out her own cell and wrote a text message. She waited at the table for another five minutes, purposefully not looking at the tank—or the body. At last the answer came: "I'll be right there. Leave everything as is—OK."

Fifteen minutes later, Rosa left the apartment. OK had his phone in his hand, talking to the police. And while Rosa went down the broad steps that led from the apartment to the Elbchaussee, she thought, *Last night . . . I should have stayed. . . .*

2. "Please close your eyes for a moment," the makeup woman said, powdering Rosa's forehead.

Again Rosa saw the stairs she'd gone down, again heard OK's voice, talking to the police, giving the address: "Elbchaussee Number . . ." And again she thought, *Why couldn't I, that one night, have stayed with her? Why did I leave?*

She leaned back, saw herself crouching in puddles on the floor in the apartment. Mira's cold body before her.

That was on the sixth of January, just one week ago.

Rosa thought, *I shouldn't have come here today.* A camera stood in front of her. The interviewer prattled something about pop starlets' short careers.

Rosa couldn't lie to herself. Here she was, in the studio. Naturally not for the money, although she needed it badly. A thousand euros, they'd offered—enough for the rent, and a few other things she could use.

The makeup woman kept fussing. A technician turned the microphone on. The sluttish interviewer burbled, "And now it's my pleasure to introduce Rosa—Mira's bosom friend."

Rosa felt like standing up and walking out. Instead she wondered, *Why did I call OK and leave it to him to call the police?* OK's first thought, of course, had been to clear out the poison cabinet. Not that it had a lot in it, mostly sleeping tablets and a few ecstasy pills. And the little plastic bottle of speed.

Now the mike was on, but the technician still messed around. He touched her neck, as though by accident. Which it wasn't, Rosa knew. The interviewer gave her a wide grin and began: "Rosa, you knew Mira well, you two played together in the sandbox, so to speak. Isn't that right?"

"Right. We were retarded, still making mud pies at fourteen."

Her voice, as always, sounded clear and bright, with a slightly scratchy undertone.

"How did you react to this tragic event?"

"How come tragic? Mira wanted to die."

"Aha . . ." The interviewer's outfit was the opposite of stylish, more like what cheap whores were wearing twenty years ago. She held her head sideways, looking like someone deep in thought, or a dog begging for food. "Rosa, the papers often mentioned depression. Do you think that caused her suicide?"

"Depression? Everybody gets depressed. You too."

"Well, Rosa, that might be. However, in an interview like this . . ." She turned to the cameraman, who knelt before her on the floor. "Hello, everyone," she gushed, "you're watching the Saturday update of *Pop Tonight*. Once again our topic is the tragic death of Mira M. Last week Mira's new song, 'Farewell,' climbed from zero to number one on the German singles charts. And no doubt," she added with a wink, "the recording company is raking in a tidy profit. . . ."

She turned back to Rosa. "Rosa, of the many rumors going around about pop stars, some start in PR departments, wouldn't you agree? There was talk of Mira's frequent stays in a psychiatric clinic. During the last few weeks of her life, would you say your friend was suicidal?"

3. No, I was not.

Even though it might have seemed that way sometimes. Like when I put the revolver on the table and suggested to Kralle, "Let's play Russian roulette"—which was wild. I mean, it was wild that I went ahead and did it. I remember the cold metal of the gun barrel against my forehead. And then the click of the cylinder like an explosion in my head.

Kralle was staring at me. I shoved the revolver toward her. She didn't take it. Without a word she got up and left the apartment. I left too, just as I was, barefoot. I crossed the Elbchaussee, ran past all those town houses, farther and farther west.

But I wasn't crazy. No, not crazy, not sick. I did have a "difficult" childhood, though—just as the papers kept saying. Papa in jail, Mama depressed—and then Uncle Lou pumping me full of tranquilizers, hiding me in his Marshall amp road case, and smuggling me across the border. At some point I woke up in black darkness and silence, weirded out and giddy from the drugs.

I was nine years old then.

According to the DSM-IV official psychological diagnostic system, I had "a nonspecific psychotic disorder." Reality

perception anomalies, to be exact. But I got out of that
clinic. And with no psycho drugs.

It wasn't "reality perception anomalies" that I had. It was
something different. There's an old people's sickness that
makes them forget things. With me it's the opposite. I
remember almost everything: my grandma's phone number
in Zagreb, getting to know Jackson, and the first recording
session in OK's studio. I remember the butterflies my grandpa
collected, the little seahorse I found on the beach near
Barcelona, the fat gray pigeon with its head smashed in, right
on the Elbchaussee. It was lying there when I ran out barefoot
late that night after I'd pushed the revolver toward Kralle.

My problem isn't memory gaps. It's that memories persist
with me, probably because I have nothing else to hold on to.

Anyway, hardly anything blurs. I always worked so long
and hard on my songs that I know which idea came to
me and which not. And this one had come to me, it was
mine. Although it wasn't such a great one, really.

I'm sorry. We did so much together, Melo and me.
Developed ideas together. But the one that caught on came
to me alone. I'd have given her co-author credit. Just so she'd
get a share of the money. But who could have known that
song would take off the way it did? Certainly not me, and not
Melody, either.

As I said, I would have let her be co-author. If she'd just
talked with me in a normal way. But she got so pissed off,
started yelling, "Are you making fun of me? Do you have it in

for people who create pop music, hoping to succeed?" Later she insisted *she'd* made up the whole refrain.

Not exactly logical.

I still replay what it was like, running into her at three a.m. at the taxi stand. Of all people, Melody. That was in November 2002, after we got back from Barcelona, playing at the MTV awards. The night when everything fell apart....

[TRACK 1]
MELODY

1. Some people are special, you feel it right away. Even as children they somehow seem grown up, unapproachable, and in school they don't really belong with the others. Sometimes they are popular, sometimes not at all.

The way they present themselves makes them unmistakable. They always stand in the center of things, whether they mean to or not. Whatever they say has particular weight, and there are always people who follow them wherever they lead.

Call it charisma. Something a person radiates. A kind of power.

And whether you have this power doesn't depend on what you do or want. You either have it or you don't.

Rosa was one of those people.

Not Melody. She wasn't ebony black like Rosa. With her light brown skin and slanted eyes she looked more Jamaican than African.

All through the tunnel she heard the echo of her heels, *clack*, *clack*, as she walked down the long platform in her dark pantsuit, the one she'd worn to the funeral. As usual she held her head just a little too straight, as though braced to answer in case anyone addressed her.

But no one saw her, the platform was deserted, the train had just pulled out. The time was noon. But here in the station it was that indefinable, somewhere-between-day-and-night time that always stays the same.

Melody stopped in front of the Hamburg public transport map. She knew perfectly well how to get to OK's apartment. Nevertheless, she studied the black lines of the different S-train routes traversing the sea of houses.

It's strange, she thought, *how we can be in one place, where we live now, and at the same time someplace completely different, where we were a long time ago.* Melody was in the Hamburg-Harburg S-train station, but also in Rose Hill, a few kilometers outside of Tema, in the south of Ghana.

She'd once read that every time you remember something, it changes a little, because you aren't remembering the original experience, but rather the memory of it. So then you just remember the memory of the memory. And so on. And it changes every time. Like when you're a kid playing Telephone, except all by yourself.

How often she'd stood in front of these neon-lit maps in S-train stations and remembered the little girl standing before the weather-beaten, ragged map with holes in it on the wooden plank wall of the store in Rose Hill. And she remembered how the sea had grown darker every day. She remembered the countries, yellow, like gas lamps. And how, like gas lamps, they had gone out.

As the platform around her again filled with people,

Melody felt herself standing in that little store with the world map on its wall. She'd stood there every day. She'd almost known that map by heart: knew where the snake turned darker blue as it swam around the Cape of Good Hope. The deeper the sea, the darker the snake, so the teacher had explained.

Melody remembered the spider that crossed from Africa to Spain. The lines that showed the ships' routes were the spider's web. And she remembered the little ants creeping over the equator. They'd made so many holes in the paper that underneath America the planks of the wall showed through. . . .

No little creatures ran over the map of Hamburg. And there was no dark blue sea. However, there was the river and the harbor.

And for this, she thought, *you risked your life. You let yourself be locked into a stinking container for cargo.* How long ago was that? Seven years! Sometimes she couldn't believe she'd been through all that to be here now and struggle on.

Yes, now she owned things she didn't have then, and surely would never have acquired back in Tema. The dark pantsuit. And the white leather boots. And yet she was the same person—the girl who'd stood before the wooden wall looking at the world map, dreaming of a ship, and also the young woman in the pantsuit who sorted letters in the Finance Ministry and struggled toward a second career because she still dreamed of becoming a singer. . . .

+ + +

Melody turned from the S-train map and checked the electronic schedule.

"Don't dream," her mother had said, pulling her away from the map of the world on the store wall. "If you want to live, you have to be awake."

But aren't we always dreaming? By day, by night? When we talk and run and think, we don't see or hear them, but the dreams are there.

She glanced up again at the arrival board. Five more minutes. The train was late. She walked over to the small kiosk and saw on the cover of *Bravo* Mira M. in a bikini, with her guitar, hair dyed blond, piled high. Mira on the covers of all the teen magazines. And on some others. Even on *Frau im Spiegel*, whose older readers had probably never heard of Mira before. On that cover, only half visible, Melody read, . . . SANG ABOUT FREEDOM AND LOVE AND ENDED IN AN AQUARIUM. The cover of another had this quote: MIRA M.: 'I AM A LIE.' And *Für Sie* inquired: DID MIRA M. LEAVE A LAST WILL AND TESTAMENT? No mention of the autopsy anywhere. Those results were not yet known.

On the cover of the *Morgenpost*, stacked next to the cash register, she read: POP STAR DEAD: NOW HER OLD FRIENDS HAVE THEIR SAY.

And, yes, Zucka had given an interview at the cemetery, right after the funeral, looking even more awkward than usual in his formal black suit, way too wide. Melody smiled. And right in front of the camera, in the middle of the interview, he'd taken out his cell phone and explained to whomever that he didn't have time just then.

At least Rosa had waited a little longer to do the *Pop Tonight* interview. Melody wondered, *Would I have, this soon?* Yes, if she'd been asked. Which didn't happen. Naturally. Mira's official friends got precedence over her official enemies.

Melody remembered a conversation from six months or so ago, when she and Mira were still able to just talk with each other. Back then Mira had told her that actually she, Mira, did *not* write her songs to be the center of attention and have everybody looking at her; no, she wrote them to hide behind, so people would understand her without actually seeing her.

That didn't exactly explain it.

That same time Mira told about hearing the voices. And about being afraid. Melody asked herself, *Why did she tell me, of all people?*

2. In all honesty, I ask myself that question too.

Melo was the exact opposite of me.

For instance, once when we were in the S-train, Melody overheard two girls talking about her.

"No way. That's not her," said one. "Is so," said the other. "I just saw her at Traxx."

Melody smiled. Yes, she'd sung at Traxx a few days before.

Melody was delighted; she loved being recognized, loved giving autographs.

Not me. That sort of thing gave me hives.

Melody thought standing in the spotlight, everyone staring at you, was fantastic.

I thought it was awful.

Here's what I really wanted in my life: three kids someday, a rich husband—I wouldn't have minded if he looked like one of the guys in Tocotronic (my all-time favorite band)—and a little house someplace where it's green. That didn't work out, I guess because I was too young....

Something else worked out: We got on the charts, with— of all my songs!—"Don't Wanna Be Famous." OK had known right away, of course. "It's got potential," was how he put it.

What Melody couldn't make happen for her in two years happened for us instantly. Without any big marketing plan. Our single took off like a rocket.

And that's how it felt, like being shot into orbit.

Later Kralle said to me, "Mira, you've aged five years in these five months." Could be. Five years in five months. A hundred fifty roller-coaster days. As though I'd known I didn't have much time left.

Naturally one changes. Toward the end the pressure was enormous. OK had invested a lot of money, and I was scared that I wouldn't be able to hold up, or that the album would flop.

Despite all that, it was fantastic. MTV put our video in rotation. The hype was on, full blast. At the tour premiere—

it was in Berlin—Rosa breezed into the dressing room, yelling, "It's crazy! People lined up along the whole street!" What we'd never expected, not even in our dreams, happened at that first concert: The audience joined in, with every song, it seemed! Even though the album wasn't out yet, only two singles. They'd downloaded the songs from the Internet. It was like a great big party, people by the thousands.

I stood at the mike, the band behind me, and it just worked. Everybody playing our thing, not even needing to look at one another. I was the music, and everyone sang, and the people in the front row reached their hands out, tried to touch me. . . .

It's only rock 'n' roll—but I like it.

Teens papered their rooms with my posters. Suddenly I got cool clothes, hand-delivered straight from the designers—free! Because I'd been transformed into a walking commercial. Whatever I wore, countless girls would be wearing very soon.

One day a brand-new Smart Cabrio stood parked under OK's posh apartment. Melody had lived there. Now I did. OK kept it to put up important musicians when they were in town for a few days. "That only happens every few months," he'd assured me, "while you're probably on tour."

"The car keys are in your mailbox. Hop in and drive it," said Zucka's message on my machine.

Anyway, I was a "celeb" now. If you looked in any newspaper, you'd see that I'd been in five places the same evening at the same time. Right . . . Sometimes we did get around like that.

+   +   +

It was a five-month roller coaster all right, going higher, always higher, so it seemed. We opened more than one case of champagne the day we got the invitation to the MTV Awards. In the middle of that night, in the middle of that high, I stood before the mirror in some club or other. All around me were girls with too much makeup on. And I looked into my face in the mirror and asked myself, *When will you hurtle down?*

I was stoned too often and let the stress and media hype get to me. . . . You could say I suffered from so-called exhaustion depression, though basically I was all right. Just sometimes I felt totally burned out, that's all. I got a prescription for that, which probably was why I miscalculated the effect of the speed. But that's another story.

Anyway, after we got back from Barcelona, when I left the Hamburg bar where we'd been celebrating and went to the taxi stand, there—at three a.m.—all of a sudden was Melody, the last person I wanted to see. For months she'd been tormenting me, insisting that *she'd* written "Don't Wanna Be Famous." When, in fact, as she'd explained to me earlier, it was a shitty song in her opinion. But, well, now that we were on the charts and all . . .

She stood in front of me, glaring. I'm so stupid, I still tried to be nice. She said, "Why don't you just pick up the phone?"

I was cold, I was tired, I'd popped too many pills. "What do you want?"

"Only what belongs to me."

"And what is that?"

"My share."

Then, alone in the taxi, I suddenly felt like talking to Kralle, couldn't find her number. Damn! I remembered deleting it the last time I got mad at her. I put the cell phone away.

The taxi radio was on, very soft, and we drove through the dark city for half an eternity. I dozed off, and every time I half awoke I heard low voices, the woman dispatcher giving street names, house numbers, interspersed with bits of talk, drivers calling in, not finding an address or name. The taxi swayed and I kept nodding off, with the radio sounds and the din from the concert buzzing in my ears.

And then in the apartment, when I lay down on the huge sofa, there were noises coming from the harbor and I told myself, *Go close the terrace door while you're still awake. Or you'll catch cold and won't sing well tomorrow.* But I stayed on the sofa, staring at the white ceiling with the silver lamps. And I heard them.

Voices. Still there. Very low, saying short, meaningless phrases, like on the taxi radio. But why was the taxi radio on, here in the apartment? I closed my eyes, opened them again. Finally I stood up and washed my face. But the voices kept on.

After a while I thought, *Maybe the TV . . . ,* because it was always on. But just then it wasn't. I walked through the large room, only half dark, because a little light came in from the Elbe. This apartment, so weird somehow. And cell phones all over the place. I tried each one, and nothing. But still the voices. I stuffed earplugs in my ears and stuck my headset on. No use. The voices continued. Saying nothing in particular, and so softly that you had to listen closely, like in the taxi. I still know what one kept whispering: "Hello ... Hello, are you still there?" Then suddenly another said, "I'm wearing a white T-shirt."

I thought, *Stay calm, Mira, you're wasted, you haven't slept in ages, you've got to really sleep.* But that didn't work. Sometimes I nodded off, but just for moments. And I lay there wide awake again, in my clothes. It was still dark out, but slowly dawn was coming. I felt like I was made of glass. The whispering kept on, right by my ear.

And it didn't stop.

[TRACK 2]
JANUARY 14, 2004

1. "Turn that thing off!"

Rosa sat ensconced in the orange swivel chair, looking paralyzed.

The metronome had been ticking to 128 beats since Zucka had found it behind the stereo and turned it on: "To test how long till it stops." That was about fifteen minutes before.

Zucka was good at finding stuff. That was about his only talent, Rosa said. Probably so. But he was really good at it. Rosa had sometimes wondered, Was there a way to make money with a talent like that?

She'd roused Zucka out of bed at eleven, early for him. "We need to find that cassette before the others come. So get yourself over here!"

"Will do." Zucka arrived, started opening drawers. When he got to the second one, he looked up and said, "A mini-cassette, you mean? Black and pink? What are those for? Kids' toys?"

"Nah, for the recorder." Rosa pushed him aside.

"Let me see what's on it."

"None of your business."

"No?"

"No."

+   +   +

Zucka left it at that. Pretended the cell phones in the upper drawer interested him more. But when Rosa took the cassette and the recorder, he watched out of the corner of his eye. And without turning around, he knew where she hid it: in the bottom compartment of the storage wall by the front door.

The metronome ticked on. Zucka scooped up the cell phones. One after the other, all over the apartment.

He also looked around for edibles. When he found something, he checked the expiration date, and if it wasn't too long ago, opened whatever it was. Just now it was a sack of pistachios. He spread the shells out on the window sill, muttering to himself.

"Camera cell phone, organizer cell phone, cheap one, genuine mother-of-pearl cell, prototype . . ."

"You're doing nicely, my sweet."

"I already found fourteen."

"All promo," Rosa said. "For free. No charge."

They only noticed Kralle when the metronome suddenly stopped. Kralle had turned it off.

"How did you get in?" Rosa asked.

"I still have the key."

"Aha," said Rosa. "You can help. Table."

Kralle looked around as though she'd never seen the

apartment, or not for a long time. She was wearing a man's suit, blue pin stripes, and over it her transparent plastic raincoat. And her red and white shoes.

A good outfit to hide her grief behind, Rosa thought. Mannish, straight lines, with a bit of irony. And still the silver rings, and the long, sharp fingernails, which were why she was called Kralle (German for "talons" or "claws").

Kralle moved as though in a trance. As though drifting in a sea of air. She approached the table and took off her coat. Rosa shot Zucka a look and said a bit too loudly, "Someone *could* set the table." Zucka didn't react. Rosa turned to Kralle and rolled her eyes. "Do we call him Zucka because he's sweet, or because he's jerky?"

"Sweetly jerky," Kralle murmured. (*Zucker* means "sugar," and *zucken*, "to jerk.")

"Is it true that men think of sex every five minutes?" Rosa asked.

Zucka looked away from the cell phones and scratched his forehead. "That could be. Maybe not punctually every five minutes. But on the average . . ."

The apartment was vast. You could have played soccer in it. It took a while to bring the dishes, glasses, and silverware from the kitchen to the table, which stood slantwise in the middle. Meantime the downstairs bell rang—tentatively. "Sounds just like her." Rosa nodded. "Melody."

Since neither Zucka nor Rosa made a move, it was Kralle who went to the door. On her way there she saw Melody on the video monitor. Wearing the dark pantsuit. Carrying two shopping bags. Pineapple fronds sticking up from one. Melo was smiling, and still smiled when she entered the apartment.

"Sorry. I'm too late."

"We know that," Rosa said.

"Can I help?"

Rosa echoed, "Comes in—I'm too late—can I help?"

Melody put down her plastic bags and started unpacking fruit.

"The train didn't come. Should I set the table?"

Rosa, back in the orange swivel chair, just shrugged her shoulders. "Comes in, grins, too late, can I help? Same old, same old . . ."

Zucka looked to Kralle for help. Kralle was trying to extricate the lasagna pan from her shoulder bag.

For a while silence reigned. There, the lasagna was out. Then, for the first time, Kralle looked Melody straight in the face and asked, "So, how's it going at the Finance Ministry?"

"Well," said Melody.

Another pause. Zucka asked, "Shouldn't we set the table?"

Melody went to the wide expanse of window and looked out at the terrace. From here she could see the Elbe, the container harbor, and beyond, all the way to the Harburg Mountains. "I used to like this view a lot," she said.

"Mmm-hmm," Rosa said.

"Those shipping-container cranes, they always look like giant storks standing on one leg—"

"When the sun goes down," Zucka added.

"Most of all when it's gray out," Melody said. "But the shipping containers, always those same small rectangles, each with its own color. Rust red, meadow green . . ." She drifted along the wide glass pane and stopped at the aquarium. She looked at the fish, shook her head, and said, "So now you two are living here?"

"No. Just looking after the fish," Zucka said.

Melody turned to Rosa.

"*I* couldn't live here now."

"No one says you should, either."

Melody looked out the window again. "What's happening with the autopsy results?"

"They have to investigate further," Rosa said. "Hair, fingernails, on account of drugs."

"Is it true that you were the last to see her?"

Rosa pointed to Zucka. "He saw her last."

"Who, me?" Zucka turned around, surprised.

"Could be," Rosa said.

"Could *not*."

"Anything could be," Melody said. "It's obvious why you were with her."

"Hello, is that obvious to everyone?" Rosa asked. She turned back to Melody. "Do you know what the difference was between Mira and you? She knew what she wanted. Didn't let herself be made a fool of. Wrote her own songs, didn't just copycat others'. You have a problem with that. And then, to go to some lawyer and accuse her, and inveigle yourself onto every talk show that is willing to hear you say you wrote that line and that one, and also this one . . ."

Melody still stood at the aquarium, but no longer tapping on the glass or watching the fish. "You know how all that gets distorted."

"Distorted? I *saw* those shows!"

"They spliced things together. I told her I was sorry."

"She told me you and she weren't talking anymore."

"I apologized on her answering machine."

"On her machine. . . ." Rosa shook her head. "First you jabbered on TV, then said you're sorry on her answering machine. . . ."

"She wouldn't talk with me," Melody said. "She hung up, didn't call back. So then I told it to her machine. . . ."

Kralle stood up and rummaged in her handbag. "Her phone did keep ringing. Off the hook." She lit a cigarette.

"A stalker . . . ," Zucka guessed.

"And now?" Rosa asked. "Why don't we all just throw up? That might help."

Melody could look daggers through a room. She was doing it now: chopping the whole giant apartment into a thousand bits. Then she said, "At least I didn't give interviews right after her death."

"Mmm-hmm," Rosa said. "Because no one's interested in you anymore."

"No?"

"It's hard, such a comedown," Rosa went on. "But it's even harder when somebody else is on the rise and gets everything you wanted for yourself. And it's hardest of all when you can't admit any of that to yourself. Because you have to be the good one. Always the good one—which can't be much fun."

"I don't have a problem with that," Melody said.

"Oh no, not much!" said Rosa. Then she turned to Kralle. "Smoking's not allowed here."

"Since when?"

"Since now."

Kralle had no intention of putting out her cigarette. She went and stood behind Rosa. "At least be honest. You and Zucka weren't interested in her anymore. Or her songs. Till 'Don't Wanna Be' sold three hundred thousand copies."

"Three hundred forty-six thousand," Zucka said.

"Then suddenly you cared, a lot. And Melody, you said *you* wrote the song," Kralle went on, "or a part, at least. The refrain. She showed me your letters. And Rosa, you went along with that. But when she had her housewarming party and invited all her friends, who came?"

"You came," Zucka said.

"She's no friend," Rosa spat.

Kralle ignored her, took a seat at the table. "And when she went to a club, just wanting to be normal again, like a regular person, and a guy standing at the bar, who now tells the papers he was her friend, didn't even say hello. Zucka, imagine, Mira comes up to you at a bar, smiles, says hi, and you just turn away."

"How should I have reacted?"

Rosa stayed calm. She swiveled around, facing Kralle.

"Yeah. And after all the false friends deserted her, you deserted her too."

Kralle shook her head. "We went to a hundred doctors, she and I. Heart problems. MRIs. Mitral valve prolapse syndrome . . . You have no idea what all Mira had."

"And you do have an idea?"

Kralle said, "Things she told no one else she confided to me."

"To me too," Rosa said.

"Me too," Zucka said.

"Me too," Melody said.

"So when is the book coming out?" Rosa asked.

"Maybe I should really write one," Kralle said.

Rosa stood up so abruptly, the swivel chair rolled backward. She went to the aquarium and almost shouted, as though wanting every word to be heard clearly in the kitchen, too. Even though no one was in there.

"Kralle, I have nothing against bad writers. Also nothing against lesbians. Or against bad lesbian writers. But people who're screwing my friend and want to write about it when she's dead . . ."

"Main thing is, that stuff sells," Melody put in.

"She doesn't belong to you," Kralle said.

"She thought she'd found a friend in you," Rosa said.

"Go ahead, write a lesbo-porn bestseller," Zucka said.

Kralle stood up, banging her knee on the table leg, and shoved the lasagna pan back into her shoulder bag. "All against Kralle?" she asked.

"All against Kralle," Rosa confirmed.

Kralle pulled on her coat. Then, limping slightly, she went to the door.

She turned around once. No one looked at her. The heavy door shut. On the small video monitor screen they could see how slowly she went down the broad stairs.

Melody stood at the wide window again. The sky was gray. Snowflakes started falling onto the cranes.

Zucka re-sorted the cell phones.

Rosa looked down, watching the fish in the aquarium.

2. So there they were.

Rosa, she was the motherly one, we always said. She'd gotten a little fat.

And Melody, who so enjoyed gazing out at the Elbe, the shipping-container harbor, the Kohlbrand Bridge. Actually, her name was Luisa.

Zucka? His real name was Paul, but he changed it to Sweet Sugar. It was Rosa who changed it to Zucker, then Zucka. He wanted to be a rapper but didn't have rhythm. So he did odd jobs in the studio for OK, his papa.

And Kralle, who went hobbling down the stairs, lips pressed tightly together.

The one not in this picture is OK himself, "the man," head
of EOK Productions: Ernst Otto Köhler—Zucka's papa, mover,
shaker, pop-star maker.

Also missing was Jackson. My great love. Got himself deported,
back to Africa. Couldn't return to Liberia where he was from,
because the war he'd fled was still going on, bloodier than ever.
Stayed in Ghana. Opened a video theater there.

The day they arrived in Hamburg—Jackson, Rosa, and
Melo—they were already famous, almost. There was an article
about them in the *Morgenpost*. Three juveniles from West
Africa, actually still children, found in a shipping container,
nearly dead from thirst: unaccompanied, underage refugees, as
they were officially called.

They'd landed on January 14, 1997. Dockworkers had
unlocked their container, with Kralle looking on.

Kralle had always been nosy. Wanted to be a writer. Lived
in a shared flat over the Shanghai Hotel on the *Reeperbahn*,
boulevard of raucous bars, tattoo salons, and such. Her real
name was Patricia, came from Ribnitz in Mecklenburg.

Me, although I'm straight, I had a thing with Kralle for a while.

If Rosa, Kralle, Melo, Zucka, and the other dreamers in my
story were like colorful aquarium fish, then OK was the eel. A
big fish, anyway. A meat eater, a carrion eater, and dangerous.
Eels have poisonous blood, acidic. That's why no one attacks
them. Eels can swim in the sea and in fresh water, they can
even wriggle over land and cross deserts.

Those are the people this is about. And naturally it's about
me. Mira M.

And the Spiders. Mira M. and the Spiders from Venus.

Most important is Kralle, at least now that I'm dead. Most
important is whoever feels the deepest grief.

Kralle, going blindly down the stairs. Seeing nothing, just the
gray steps under her feet.

The others, all against Kralle. When it was Kralle who had
helped. Seven years ago, when Melo, Rosa, and Jackson first
landed in Germany. If it hadn't been for Kralle, they wouldn't
be here anymore. Officially speaking, they wouldn't even have
arrived.

Kralle, it's me! Do you feel the snowflakes dancing down
from the sky and melting in your hair?

Oh, all right, keep running.

Sometimes it's better just to run.

And not turn back. To see nothing. To feel nothing. To not
think about things anymore.

Just now a snowflake, soft as butter, has landed on your
pointy nose. Your pointy nose, which I always loved.

Kralle . . . You did too much for others. People who do
too much for others end up getting kicked in the ass for
thanks.

Anyway: When Kralle left, and the others stayed in the
apartment, I'd have gladly switched channels and watched
something else. But you can't.

Rosa, Melo, and Kralle—a great combination, but very volatile. When they stormed onto a dance floor, imitating different dance styles from the moonwalk to Britney Spears and giving hunky guys the eye, they were camera-ready, a sight to behold.

Other times, when they quarreled, they were like little girls at one another's throats about whose Barbie doll is the prettiest.

I always liked our anniversary feasts on January 14. Kralle made lasagna. With lots of cheese, from Penny's Supermarket. Rosa cooked African banku. Zucka brought cheap wine in cartons. Melody brought fruit.

But on this occasion I would not have wanted to be there. I'd have liked to spare myself the sight.

Those who commit suicide get punished once they're dead. So people say. I've always wondered, what makes people think they know?

There's something to it, though. You don't actually get punished here. It's more like a work assignment: You *have to* listen in whenever those you left behind are talking about you. From start to finish. In real time. You can't fast-forward, or save it for later.

Of course I've said it wasn't suicide. Probably everyone says that. I know, it looked damn close. And from a certain point of view, maybe that's what it was.

+   +   +

Everyone does it—that's how it looks from up here. Because
thinking about suicide means you want to die. And everyone
wants to, sooner or later. To really live forever—who wants
that? Who could bear it? I say, at one moment or another, all
human beings decide to die. To systematically strangle their
selfhood and their lives. They just don't call it suicide, they call
it growing up. Being reasonable, realistic. Accepting what they
must. Functioning.

Welcome to the machine.

Naturally all this is also true of me. But a suicide in the
literal sense I'm not. I hope I'll be able to make that clear.

Anyhow—it's exactly as you imagine. Anybody thinking
about suicide imagines what others will say about it.

And now I know why you imagine it: Because that's how
it really is. You sit here and you listen. Of course you don't
really sit, or stand, or lie flat, because you have no body here,
therefore no bodily position. But spiritually, in your soul—and
that is what counts—it feels as though you're sitting on some
shabby sofa, watching reality TV.

You just can't fidget or get a beer or go to the john.

So I watch Kralle going down the broad stairs, heading into
the snow.

She stops, cranes her neck, closes her eyes. She opens
them again and looks into the sky, into the snowflakes
tumbling toward her.

The same way she now looks into the sky, that's how
she'd looked at me back then. The night I slid the revolver
toward her. Speechless. Uncomprehending.

+   +   +

There were times you could have thought, Mira's off her
rocker. Like when I got jealous. Jealousy was one thing I just
couldn't handle. It shook me up; it threw me. Kralle said that
other woman she was seeing meant nothing to her. And I
knew she wasn't lying. Even so, it drove me nuts. Never mind
that I myself had something going on the side. With that
dopey Snowflake guy.

Kralle loved me, so she said.

Love doesn't exist, only self-love.

And jealousy.

But then why did I propose Russian roulette? "If you really
love me, prove it." Oh man, pure kitsch. I got the revolver
from the kitchen drawer. The cold metallic smell of the barrel
against my forehead. The click of the cylinder. Kralle's eyes
staring at me. I slid the revolver over to her, knew it had a
bullet in it.

Kralle didn't pick it up.

And I thought, *If she leaves, I'll go with that guy Snowflake.*
Whom I didn't love. As though you could trade in one person
for another, just like that.

I wasn't crazy, wasn't sick. Just dumb.

[TRACK 3]
MEMORIES ARE MADE
OF THIS

1. But maybe that's just Kralle's role: helping other people one hell of a lot and getting kicked for it.

Other people, like Melo and Rosa, and, yes, also me.

Eight years ago I'd just come to Hamburg. I asked at the soup kitchen about a place to crash. And Kralle took me with her, to Altenwerder. To the *Bauwagenplatz*—a field of shacks and trailers where the hippies lived.

Of the village Altenwerder there was nothing left, just a church and a graveyard. Everything else had been torn down to make room for the shipping-container park.

I'd been on the road half a year; I was kaput. Going back to Uncle Lou was out of the question. I was glad to have someplace to stay. Even if it was just a trailer.

Naturally, I wasn't sleeping with Kralle back then. It was 1996. I was a tender fourteen, trying to figure out who I was. Kralle just helped me, that's all. No strings attached. She made me understand that I had to at least call Uncle Lou, let him know I was still alive. Then get hold of some ID. Money for rent. Social assistance. School. She organized all that and got me registered officially as staying with one of those alternative teachers in Altona, which gave me a legitimate address—which the *Bauwagenplatz* is not.

Slowly I adjusted. And then one day Kralle vanished. Went to the railroad tracks around the container loading zones to pick up firewood. And didn't come back.

It wasn't like Kralle to vanish.

The next day we started to worry, me and the long-haired hippies there—worry about her because it was ice-cold, the dead of winter, and also about ourselves.

Because now, who'd take care of us?

2. Kralle had heard the knocking. It came from inside one of the shipping containers.

She leaned her bike against the stump of a sawed-off birch tree and climbed to the highest point of the grass-stubbled hill.

There she crouched, and looked toward the containers. They were frost-covered, like the whole landscape. The wind had bent the bushy grass almost to the ground. She pulled the zipper on her green parka all the way up.

Then she saw the workers coming from behind one container. They knocked on the metal side. A knocking answered: three short knocks, three long ones, three short.

Three times short, three times long, three times short. Save our souls. SOS.

One of the workers started running, disappeared from view. Kralle crept into a thicket. Even without leaves, it hid her pretty well. She started to roll a cigarette, which wasn't easy because her hands were stiff from the cold. Then she realized she didn't have a light and stuck the rolling paper into her tobacco pouch.

After about fifteen minutes the worker who'd run off came back, followed by the police. Waterfront police, Kralle could tell by their uniforms. They surrounded the container. Then more workers came, with tools. There was a padlock that had to be smashed open.

Meantime a police minibus appeared on the field path. Kralle crept deeper into the thicket. She looked toward the container again and saw the door opening.

The boy was fifteen at most. It was harder to guess the girls' ages. One seemed already grown up, maybe because she looked more solid and strong.

All three wore thin pants and T-shirts, no jackets, not even sweaters. They shivered like fish in a bucket. They were hurried into the police bus. The workers entered the container, holding their noses.

At first Kralle didn't get what was happening, couldn't connect the facts of what she'd seen in a logical way. Waterfront police, African juveniles in a shipping container, handcuffs. She just followed her instinctive dislike of uniformed officials and sensed a task awaiting her, something important she needed to do.

She ran to her bike, rode over the bumpy grass to the path, and followed the police bus as it speeded ahead. Pretty soon all she could see was a little greenish-white dot turning right onto the street, heading for the Elbtunnel.

After a few hundred meters she gave up the chase. Impossible to catch up to a minibus on her rusty old bike. But when she reached the street and looked over to the *Autobahn*, she saw that one of the lanes to the tunnel had been closed off. Traffic was jammed, backed up so far that, even on foot, she could easily have caught up.

She couldn't ride her bike through the tunnel, but what she could do was take the ferry to Hamburg. From Teufelsbrück it was only a few minutes to the Othmarschen exit. She'd catch up with the minibus there.

3. Rosa, Jackson, and Melody, who was still Luisa then, had slipped into the shipping container on December 30, 1996. On the night of December 31, the ship left the harbor of Tema in southern Ghana. The three of them had no idea how long the trip would take.

They didn't know one another.

Aside from the little they'd brought along, the only things in the container were two cartons of small water bottles. One bottle for every day, the man had said. But he hadn't said if that meant one bottle for each, or for them all to share.

First they'd thought more people would join them, maybe a grown-up or two. But the container stayed closed. Then the loading began.

They didn't know where the ship was headed. Jackson thought America. "My mind tells me so," he said.

Rosa and Melody didn't believe him, because the man who'd sold them their places said they were going to France.

The first few days it was hot. There was no toilet, not even a pail. They decided to eat and drink very little, so they could hold it in till they arrived. But after a few days they couldn't anymore. They put a blanket over the mess.

After ten days the water bottles were empty. Melody said people can last for six days, if they're healthy. They decided to stick it out for five, then knock for help.

Thirst set in. At some time or other, they started talking about how many days had passed. At least two, they figured. But maybe four or five. They crouched in the dark and heard the ship's engines humming. And always water dripping outside. As though someone meant to remind them of their thirst.

Jackson grew feverish. Melody and Rosa, too, lay there half asleep, half unconscious. They couldn't have said for how long.

Noise awoke them.

Everything in motion. Freezing cold. The container shaking this way and that. Jackson was so scared, he cried. Melody comforted him.

At some time it grew quiet. No more engine noises, just a soft singing sound. And the sound of water dripping. For hours. That's when they started to knock on the metal wall of the container. When they heard the dockworkers' voices, they thought of what the man had said: "If they find you, they'll throw you into the sea."

+   +   +

And now they sat in the back of a police minibus.

Rosa looked out the barred window at this strange for-
eign place. All she saw were containers, every color: marine
blue, shiny white, rust red, meadow green. And little eight-
wheelers, heavily loaded, with orange blinkers, scurrying
among them like ants.

It was a city of shipping containers, and in between them,
gray expanses of water. Above, a gray sky glowing fiery gold
in the west.

There were so many that Rosa thought this had to be the
destination of all the shipping containers in the world.

So, of course, she and the others had landed here, in
this city of containers, and not in France, as the man had
promised. She could tell by the language that they weren't
in France. She'd picked up a few French expressions when
she'd crossed through Ivory Coast, traveling from Liberia to
Tema.

And Melody agreed, clearly this wasn't France.

Jackson sat up straighter and said in a weak voice, "I told
you we were going to America."

"America?" One of the officers turned around and laughed.

4. As the waterfront police saw it, this matter had gotten
off to a bad start. Their guidelines were quite specific:
Stowaways had to be informed while still aboard ship that
they would be deported. There was great legal significance
in this.

But when these three juveniles were released from the

container, they set foot on German soil. That fact complicated everything. It meant they'd entered the *Bundesrepublik*, which automatically gave them certain rights.

From there on things proceeded according to the rule book. They were brought to the waterfront police precinct, made to answer nineteen items on official questionnaires and sign the document of consent confirming that they'd been informed that they would be "deported via airplane."

Then the required entry forms had to be filled out, fingerprints and photos taken, authorized insurance agents notified, and authorized doctors summoned, mainly to estimate the three stowaways' ages. This was essential because the child protection convention regulations only applied to illegals under the age of sixteen.

Then Jackson, who could hardly stand up, was taken to a hospital; Rosa and Melody were bussed to a jail where illegals were interrogated.

They'd been delivered to a bureaucracy that had only one goal: to deport them as fast as possible. Normally, without someone to tell them where and when to apply for what, their chances of staying in Germany would have been nil.

But Kralle had caught sight of the police bus in Othmarschen and chased it all through the evening rush hour into the inner city. Then she spent hours at the precinct, insisting that somebody talk to her.

Well after dark, she was finally told which hospital and jail the stowaways had been taken to.

[TRACK 4]
COUNTRY ROADS,
TAKE ME HOME

1. For three days and nights it was as though Kralle had been sucked down into the earth. She hadn't even really shut the door of her trailer. I knew where she'd gone—to the railroad tracks in the container harbor, where you could always find boards and planks used in the loading process. Those were nice and dry, made first-rate firewood. I followed before it got dark. But there was no sign of her.

To be honest, I got along just fine in the *Bauwagenplatz*, even with Kralle missing. Somehow, for me, it was—this may sound corny—a magical place. Exactly what I had always looked for.

Sometimes it's like when you're reading a novel, and you suddenly lose the thread. You leaf back. To find out where you came from. And where not. You leaf back. . . .

To a street of row houses in Yugoland, Zagreb. I and the other children had the run of the neighborhood. Our playgrounds were demolition sites, meadows, industrial areas.

Sometimes you stumble onto something, and everything is changed. It was a place I found:

A car cemetery, or call it a junkyard, with a decrepit fence around it . . .

An old man used to drive his rickety old truck through our neighborhood and the surrounding villages, picking up discarded auto parts and tires, and sometimes he brought them here.

The place was a flattened-out hollow, with a couple of trees and rusty iron lying all around. The first time I came here with the other kids, late one afternoon, sunbeams slanted through the leaves and lit up the iron, made it gleam.

The other kids ran to a big old wreck of a truck and played on it. I stood still. I was around six years old. And I knew: Here it was. My just-right place. The grass, the trees, the sky, the big black tires, and behind it hills all the way to the horizon.

I sat in the yellow grass. "Here it is," I said softly to myself. I lay down, face on the cool ground.

I was happy and I knew: I don't need more than this.

The other kids came here once in a while. I came every day. I found a big tire I could sit in. The man with the truck didn't see me. No one did. No one knew this hiding place.

Later I knew that I would find this place again sometime, somewhere—or anyway, a place that was just simply right. And thanks to Kralle I found it again in the *Bauwagenplatz* in Altenwerder with the hippies.

I was thirteen when I split, left Uncle Lou's. Not that I'd actually decided to. I just did it.

He was having one of his rage attacks. He screamed and screamed at me for standing in the wrong place at the wrong time—blocking his light while he noodled around on his guitar.

More likely the real reason was I'd asked him for money, a few mark, and that was what set him off.

He screamed in my ear for I don't know how long. Finally his girlfriend pulled him away, because she felt sorry for me. Also because they were supposed to be someplace that evening and she wanted to get going.

When they were gone, I took my sleeping bag out of a closet. I figured I'd traveled around so much with them, I'd do fine on my own. I took my savings account book and a hundred mark from the touring cash box. Aside from that I took nothing, not my guitar, not my mother's brooch. I didn't feel like dragging any old stuff along.

When I stood outside I looked at the little house with its front garden and silently said, *So long.*

Thumbing rides to who-knew-where was like a long, drawn-out dream. I woke up a few times, looked around, Oh, so here's where I am. . . . Every few days a new city. Needing somewhere to crash and get something to eat. When I was lucky I'd find a guy I could stand, some nice old punk rocker who'd take me in for a while.

After six months I was a mess. I had nightmares from sniffing glue, I had scabies, and I was hungry. But I would never go back to Uncle Lou.

And here's how I got to know Kralle: She was barefoot, just like me. So I spoke to her.

I still remember sitting behind her on her rusty bike. It was that time of year called old wives' summer, when leaves, golden yellow, drifted down off trees, and we bumped along across a field path.

Kralle explained the whole business about Altenwerder, that it used to be a neat village of snug little houses at the edge of Hamburg, and then they'd started to expand the harbor, the container harbor. That's why this whole area had no more people, not even regular streets anymore, just a church, a graveyard, and a few shacks and trailers.

Riding along, I had to hold on tight to Kralle, and to my sleeping bag and shoulder bag. We were laughing, and we sang, "Country roads, take me home, to the place I belong. . . ."

Riding past a huge pile of construction wreckage . . . that's when I saw the crudely nailed-together shacks with smoking stovepipes. The trailers. In the middle of them all was a fire pit. Around them, trees, behind them, a few hills.

And that's when I knew it.

I'd found my place again. The place I'd been looking for, ever since I was a kid.

I liked living there. As I said, ten horses could not have dragged me back to Uncle Lou, and I was happy to have someone like Kralle helping me with complicated things, especially with the Youth Bureau. So it wasn't too great when Kralle suddenly vanished. She was my main support. Besides, we were out of firewood, and I didn't have a bike to ride to go pick up more from around the railroad tracks. So I had to scrounge, and beg the hippies to lend me some.

+   +   +

Three days later, suddenly, there she was again. Totally
preoccupied, didn't even say hello. It was by chance that I even
saw her. I was passing by her trailer, and the door stood open,
even though I'd closed it.

Back then Kralle didn't wear vintage pinstripes from the
sixties or a see-through plastic coat. She wore a shabby green
parka, roomy work pants patched all over, and a thick woolen
scarf around her head. That's how I'd always imagined the
women who joined the Yugo partisans in World War II.

She stood hunched over, rummaging in the crate she kept
old clothes in. I ran to her, overjoyed that she was back, but
she ignored me. Pulled out a sweater. It had big holes in it.
Shook her head, stuffed it back in. At other times something
like that hadn't bothered her.

Then she talked, not too coherently, about winter clothes
urgently needed, and what a pain it was, dealing with
bureaucrats, having to fill out reams of aliens' forms, and about
a shipping container. I couldn't make heads or tails of it.

This was during Kralle's highly political period, and it wasn't
the first time she'd done battle with what she called "official
bureaucrap."

She stuck some old sweaters and jackets into a plastic
bag, got back on her bike, and said she was going to the
laundromat.

That's how it went for the next few days. She'd appear for a
short while, not paying attention to anything else in her life.
One time she asked me, "Do you want to come along?"

"Where to?"

"To a meeting about some initiative," she said breathlessly, "and then to the deportation jail."

I said no. That politico-crap was not my thing.

[TRACK 5]
LOVE WILL FIND A WAY

1. I didn't meet my future "bosom friend" Rosa, nor my future closest enemy Melo, and also not Jackson until four weeks after they'd landed. Because they had no valid documents, it took that long to clear up the momentous question of how old they were. Sixteen or older, they'd have been put on the next plane and deported. But they were lucky. They received limited-stay permission.

After the hospital, Jackson was placed in communal housing for unaccompanied juvenile refugees, male; Melody and Rosa, ditto, female. They went to a school at the other end of the city that offered a special class on assimilation. And once a week they had to report to the Aliens Bureau to get their permits renewed.

Kralle went to see them regularly. Finally she invited all three to visit her.

They'd probably imagined that Kralle's place would be different. Or maybe they hadn't imagined it at all.

I was sitting by the fire pit with my guitar when they appeared from behind the wreckage pile.

If you knew Rosa and Melo today, you wouldn't believe what they'd looked like. Now Rosa is the project manager at EOK Productions. Back then she hardly knew German and wore a shapeless old sweater from Kralle's collection. And Jackson . . . he was only just fifteen.

Kralle proudly led the way. They followed, looking around, bewildered. Well, actually no more bewildered than most people who never saw a *Bauwagenplatz* before. Even if they don't say it, there's a big question in their eyes: You live here? But Rosa, Melo, and Jackson were bewildered in another way too: I mean, if you're coming from a harbor town in Ghana to advanced, high-tech Hamburg, and you see a place like this . . . I said hello, but I was intent on a song, didn't want to be distracted. Kralle took them to the cooking trailer to make tea. And I focused on my guitar.

Another important change in my life I owed to living there: I started to make music again. Since that scene with Uncle Lou I hadn't touched a guitar. If musicians were egomaniacal assholes like him, then I didn't feel like becoming one. Besides, when you're on the road, you don't get much chance to practice.

But the *Bauwagenplatz* hippies had a band, and three of them played electric guitar. They could do solos, really long ones, and repeated them in every song. But they weren't good at playing real rhythm guitar. I couldn't stand it for long. I'd already played electric guitar when I was eleven, probably because that was the way to get recognition from Lou. And I'd already written a few songs of my own. My first love song I composed at age twelve. It had exactly two chords: E minor and A minor. Now, suddenly, I felt inspired again. Because spring was in the air.

And also because one morning Kralle, coming back from who knows where, said, "Surprise!" and handed me a guitar, not shiny new, but with a smooth, rich sound.

Winter in that place was rough. I still remember when you woke up in the morning the rags that Kralle'd hung over the windows were frozen stiff. You shivered, lighting the stove. And if you'd used up the wood overnight, you had to go out into the icy wind and get more.

In spring it was great. You went outside and stood in the middle of a meadow, under trees. You heard birds twittering— well, anyway, crows cawing. . . .

I stayed by the fire pit drinking coffee, and I wrote a song. A sad ballad, because a while ago, before I got to this place, something had happened with a guy, and it still haunted me.

Kralle sat in the cooking shack drinking tea with Rosa and company. I kept on diddling with my song. One ride I'd hitched took me to Essen, and there I fell head over heels for a young punk rocker, and now I needed a course of self-therapy. The first two refrain lines went like this:

You won't understand me
Not in a thousand years . . .

I couldn't get any further, so I repeated the first stanza a couple of times. Then I gazed at the charred wood in the fire pit. And felt the balmy air of spring around me. I didn't look up till a raindrop hit the back of my neck.

That's when I saw him.

Years later, sometimes, I'd raise my eyebrows in that special way he had, and I'd remember:

That was Jackson.

He looked at me in a shy, attentive way.

I played a few more chords, searching for how the song might go. I always worked on my songs in that determined, dogged way.

No use. I had to look up again.

Jackson had a soft face. . . . Nicely defined nose, almond-shaped eyes. He looked friendly, and somehow also witty. His hair stood straight up. It was too short for an Afro.

Raindrops fell a little faster. He wiped some off the back of his neck, looked up, then at me, then away again, and pulled on the hood of his sweatshirt.

I started to put the guitar in its case.

And suddenly I had the idea, and sang softly, to myself:

You won't understand me,
Not in a thousand years.
I won't see you again,
Not if I cry a thousand tears
Like how we were
On that first night,
Both of us there,
The time was right.
And now I can't go on,
Not anywhere. . . .

Something amazing happened: an image like two photos superimposed. On one, the face of the fifteen-year-old punk rocker I had a tragic romance with. On the other, Jackson. I could see them both at once. Then Jackson's face came more and more into the foreground. But the other didn't quite disappear. So I already knew how this would end.

I was glad he didn't ask what was I doing, what was the song about, and had I made it up myself? He just looked at me with his big brown eyes, then looked away again, at the ground, at the sky.

It was raining pretty hard. We looked at each other and smiled, and I saw the raindrops landing on his nose. . . .

Love comes and finds its way.

Nobody can prevent it.

Well, to clear that up: In the final analysis, lovers make chemical connections, we're couples whom chance throws together. We're attracted or repelled. Antigens or not.

It's possible that Jackson had no idea what it did to me when he raised his eyebrows his special way and looked at me so shyly. He didn't know what flirting means. He was so not like those black guys in the S-train who come on to you.

He looked around, then said, "This is a nice place."

I looked around too—saw raindrops dancing in the puddles, drumming softly on the new leaves. Then I looked down at the fire pit, up at the clouds growing thicker and thicker, and finally at him.

+   +   +

I'd just turned fourteen. And he was fifteen at most.

Scientists have discovered that at this age hormones paralyze the brain. Somehow the nerve endings aren't closed off. So the nerves are exposed, they're hypersensitive. That's why the brain doesn't work right. It's like we're not fully conscious.

Exactly as nature intends. Here is the reason for hormones: to make us unaware. And why does nature want that? So we'll fall on each other and have sex, till the children come.

And then there's love. Love results if my genetic code and his genetic code fit together, making for optimal progeny. Genetic code determines what my nose looks like, or my ear. And the nose has receptors that can determine whose genetic code fits mine. The code says which two people attract each other. If two people do, love happens. Antigens or not. Either you can smell each other or you can't. And your intelligence has to figure it out. Or not.

I don't know what Jackson thought. Anyway, the rain seemed not to bother him. Nor that it was getting chilly out here.

I asked him, "Want to go inside?" and pointed to the cooking trailer. A burned-down candle flickered in the window.

Kralle had lit the stove. It was toasty in there. So that was when I got to know Rosa, and Melody, who was still Luisa. Much later the three of them became the "trio infernale" and made every party rock. Back in the trailer they looked uncomfortable and awkward, squeezed together. There wasn't

a whole lot of room. Rosa fussed with her sweater. They'd
only just started learning German. Conversation didn't exactly
flow.

Pretty soon they had to leave to get back on time to their
residences for underage illegals. Jackson and I—we made a
date for the next day.

So began our love story. Which I'll skip for now.

2. Because three weeks later, courtesy of Easy, a computer
program that mathematically determined who should go
where, Jackson, Rosa, and Melody were scheduled to be
"relocated"—Rosa to Schleswig-Holstein; Melody to Bavaria;
and Jackson to Mecklenburg-Pomerania. To tiny hick towns
probably chock full of neo-Nazis.

Kralle got right on it, moved heaven and earth to keep
this from happening. I did too. Suddenly that politico-crap
interested me a lot, and I ran along to various authorities and
lawyers, and we finally succeeded.

That was when we decided that no matter what, wherever
our destinies led us, we'd have a big anniversary feast every
year. On the fourteenth of January. To celebrate the day
when Rosa, Melo, and Jackson had heard the dockworkers'
voices. And Kralle had gone looking for firewood along
the railroad sidings. And I'd huddled, freezing cold, in the
Bauwagenplatz, alone. On January 14...

When we made that decision, we five were still children: Rosa,
Melo, Jackson, Kralle, and me. Later Zucka came along. We

held the first anniversary feast in the *Bauwagenplatz*; the next two, in Kralle's pad on the *Reeperbahn*. And from then on, in the huge apartment.

We were children, but also a family: Rosa, the mama; Kralle, the papa; Melo, the daughter; Zucka, the son; and me, Mira, the little sister they'd adopted because I seemed so sweet and vulnerable. And Jackson—except the others kept forgetting about him.

Now I know it. Everything that happened only happened because we loved one another. Like in most tragedies. If we'd all been indifferent, hadn't cared, our lives wouldn't have gotten so hard.

But that's how it was.

Jackson was not the only one to fall in love with me back then. Kralle already had, then Rosa, then Melo too, insofar as she could. They fell in love with me.

And they loved Mira to death.

That's what Kralle thought, after she . . .

[TRACK 6] JANUARY 14, 2004: PART TWO

1. After she closed the apartment door behind her and rushed down the steps, Kralle walked for thirty minutes, not noticing anything around her. When she finally looked up, she saw snow flurrying in whirling whiteness that grew thicker and thicker. The river and the opposite shore had already disappeared from view.

The snowstorm seemed to stand before her like a wall. She kept walking . . . and all around her was a blizzard so cold that even the flakes on her face did not melt.

She went down a few stairs to the Elbe and tramped on through snow that now was sticking to the gray, sandy shore.

Kralle asked herself when she had last seen the sun. At the cemetery, of course. Ever since November there'd been rain and wet snow; just on that one January day the sun had shone, and the air had warmed as if it was spring.

Kralle thought of the small chapel, the smell of wax, and the musty, damp walls of the place, the gleaming wooden coffin slowly disappearing into a door that swung open. The coffin was incinerated, the ashes placed in an urn, the urn buried. And somewhere in there, supposedly, was Mira.

A priest spoke, Carlo from the band played organ music, and the faces all around looked dead, deader than Mira's ashes in the urn.

Kralle asked herself, *What happens after? Is there such a thing as a soul that departs from the body and lives on, wherever?*

Kralle clung to her belief in people's goodness. But she remembered standing before Mira's little grave, maybe one meter square, and shuddering. She had a horrible feeling that everyone around her wore a mask. Except maybe OK. The corners of his mouth hung down in suitable sadness, but the rest of his fat face expressed his usual self-satisfaction. The others were stony-faced, eyes lowered to the ground. What were they looking for? They really didn't want to look there at all, Kralle thought grimly. It's just that they were afraid to look up, because then their looks would meet, they'd have to look in one another's eyes. Some had frozen smiles on, and Melody cried quietly. But their faces concealed what they were really feeling. As though they had plaster-of-Paris masks on—which Kralle felt like tearing off.

How could it be that a person was here and then not anymore? Walking along the bank of the Elbe, through the snow that was melting now, Kralle had a feeling, a certainty, that Mira would pop up around the next corner with her black woolen hat on, smiling, holding a cigarette. She thought of these lines in a song, Mira's favorite: "Rock 'n' Roll Suicide":

Time takes a cigarette
Puts it in your mouth
You pull on your finger, then another finger
Then your cigarette . . .

Maybe Mira wasn't a rock 'n' roll suicide, but the fact was that for her, the height of fame had also been the depth of loneliness.

On the sixth of January, when Kralle heard on the radio that Mira had died, her first thought was, *No!* This had to be PR from EOK Productions. Because OK's concept all along had been to meld Mira's personal history with her public image and cannibalize it. And Mira had gone along with it: Princess out of nothingness. Childhood in an industrial town in Yugoslavia, father jailed for political reasons, the little girl doped up with narcotics, smuggled out of the country in a guitar amp case.

A fabulous story for the media, especially because that little girl was now a cool young woman. This one image— the child, hidden in a Marshall amp road case inside a Yugo rock band bus and smuggled into Germany—had become emblematic of Mira M. The amp case kept appearing in her first, very simply produced video, turning and floating around in space while she tried to climb inside it and hide.

Kralle kept walking westward, aimlessly. Wind blew in her face, the seagulls screeched, and it took a while before she noticed her cell phone ringing.

Once she saw Zucka's name on the display she didn't want to answer. But oddly, the message didn't flash, and the cell kept ringing.

"Zucka?"

"Yes."

She trudged over the sand.

"Kralle . . . ," he stammered.

"Yes?"

He too seemed not to know what to say. Finally: "I'm standing out here on the terrace, smoking."

"Fine."

"Yes, really fine. I can see the Elbe, the shore . . ."

"And me?"

"Where are you, anyway?"

"Already past Övelgönne."

"Nah, can't see that far from here."

"Is that why you're calling?"

Zucka stayed silent for another moment.

"Kralle. You know how Rosa is," he said then.

Kralle walked silently on.

"You know how she means something like that."

Kralle deliberated whether to say no. Or yes. Or nothing at all. Or whether she should scream, loudly, into the receiver.

"Kralle . . ."

"Umm?"

"Rosa's just totally done in, kaput. Like we all are."

"Yes. Well . . ."

"Since Mira . . . Since she . . ."

"You mean, since she died?"

"Yes."

"And?"

"Since . . . We're all in bad shape. So that's why we sometimes say things we don't mean."

"Rosa most of all."

"Most of all Rosa. You know how she is."

"Yes, I know her."

"She doesn't mean it the way it sounds."

"Then how?"

Zucka pulled on his cigarette.

"Kralle . . . I've been thinking. Let's agree on something."

"On what?"

"That we here, the friends of Mira, won't reproach ourselves about her death. So that we don't demolish one
another."

Kralle grasped why Rosa and Zucka had come to the apartment. And also what Melody was looking for there. It wasn't
to relive old memories.

Kralle had no desire to be with them again, in that
gigantic, underfurnished space with the corpselike smell in
the air.

The worst thing was that all the friendship and affection
there'd been among them still existed, but were not wanted
anymore.

Thinking about that, Kralle imagined she could make
everything all right again—a fantasy she'd had since

childhood. When something had gone wrong at home, she'd thought of ways to solve it. One time, when her mother had no money at all to buy food, Kralle went around to all the stores and asked if they had work for her. She was just twelve at the time. She said she was fourteen so she could get a paper route, and then secretly stashed the money she earned in the housekeeping box.

Thinking about it now, she could hardly believe it herself. But that's how it was. And it didn't mean she was an angel, either. A few years later she secretly took money out of that same box. And she didn't have the paper route for long, because she couldn't manage to get up at six o'clock every morning.

But she dreamed this dream again and again: that she could work things out, make everything be all right, and not tell anyone at all that she'd done it. Then everybody would be happy again.

With Mira, too, she'd just wanted to help.

But she hadn't been able to, any more than the others.

For an instant Kralle saw Mira's face before her, smiling, and saw the revolver her friend held out to her.

"If you want me to believe you, then you'll do it."

The revolver looked pretty heavy. It weighed down Mira's hand as she laid it on the table, then slid it over to Kralle.

Of course it had been right not to take the thing.

But was it also right to leave? To stand up and abandon Mira without saying a word?

Maybe sometimes staying was better. Or going back, if you'd already left. Even if everything in you rebelled at the idea.

This last thought made Kralle stand still a moment. She looked at the Elbe; then she turned around.

[TRACK 7]
CHILDHOOD DREAMS

Kralle didn't understand me.

I didn't either.

But this much I knew about myself: I specialized in having fits. Even when I was little. I'd sit quietly for hours, just playing make-believe in a corner. Then suddenly some little thing would set me off. For instance, one time my mother brought me a doll I didn't like. And I ran out of the apartment so furious, I threw myself down the stairs. I still have a little scar on my chin from that.

Another time, at my grandma's, I wrecked half her kitchenware because I'd made myself a sandwich, and my cousin had helped himself to it. I suddenly felt burning hot, everything got foggy around me, I was dizzy and started smashing things. Afterward I didn't remember what I'd done.

Uncle Lou thought I had high blood pressure, plus, he said, "the Serbian temperament." This good-looking psychologist I went to later said something about borderline personality. Borderline people live right on the edge, between normal and falling apart. Because they can't recognize any borders in themselves.

It's impossible to understand another person. The truth is, you can't even understand yourself. The only thing you can grasp—

maybe—is where you come from, what and who made you become as you are: housing project, school, Mama, Papa, Oma.

Sometimes, when I was by myself in the *Bauwagenplatz*, plinking around on the guitar, I'd let one hand sag down while my other still clutched the guitar, and blur my eyes, and a memory would come. A picture inside me from years before, indistinct, gray on gray and very still.

I myself was never in such pictures, nor were other children. Or any other people. Just places. Streets, houses, hills.

Squinting, I'd make out a big building, sort of a skyscraper in Zagreb where my father had worked. When my mother and I picked him up from there, I'd stay down at the entrance while she went in to ask for him.

It was the administration part of an important factory. He managed that factory, which made synthetic fabrics. This was when there still was a Yugoslavia, around 1990. I'd just started school.

Then one day the Croats declared they weren't part of Yugoslavia anymore; they said they'd rather have their own state. The problem was that lots of Serbs lived in Croatia. Some neighborhoods in Zagreb were almost entirely Serbian.

And suddenly all the Serbs were supposed to leave. The Croats started their own army, so the Serbs did too. And then a war broke out in the middle of Europe, and people who'd lived in peace together for decades started killing their neighbors.

Most Serbs who'd had important positions left Croatia, went to Belgrade. But not my father. He didn't want to. For a while he stayed on as head of the factory, because he'd been so successful. Then he lost the job. The president of Croatia personally offered to pay him a settlement and transfer him to Serbia, but my father refused. He wasn't political. He just wanted to stay. Finally he was accused of industrial espionage and got arrested.

Meantime, Serbian planes were bombing Croatian cities. People on the streets didn't speak to us anymore, and when we went shopping, storekeepers wouldn't sell us anything.

Papa sat in jail, Mama cried every day. When I think of my childhood, I think of the kitchen that was totally neat and where nothing got cooked, and Mama sitting at the sparkling clean table, weeping.

But she wasn't put in the clinic until I was living with my grandma. She didn't have any money either, and we took the bus to the country and bought food from farmers. Oma cooked all day long, and I wasn't allowed out.

I think it was back then that I started feeling that something was wrong with me. That I was less than the others. Not that I was littler or worse, just simply less.

Not that I was treated especially badly. I wasn't treated any way at all. I simply had nothing to do with the other children in the apartment house. And I didn't play with them, because they did awful things. The boys peed in the elevator and sometimes into people's mailboxes. That wasn't so easy, because you had to climb up to do it.

Oma explained to me that I was much too sensible to play such awful games, and I agreed.

At school I took it for granted that nobody was interested in me. Whether I was there or not didn't matter. My grandma was the only person I sometimes played with: Fisherman, Fisherman, How Deep Is the Water, or Black Peter. Mostly I played on my own. What I loved best was the butterflies. Before my grandpa died, he'd started a collection.

Sometimes my mother got sent home from the clinic; then I went back to her. The apartment wasn't so polished and neat anymore. There'd be wine bottles and full ashtrays everywhere, and empty medicine vials in the bathtub. My mother gulped down loads of pills for headaches. But the headaches only got worse. And she still sat at the kitchen table, weeping.

When I was little, my mother was a pretty woman. Now she'd gotten fat and mostly wore a long T-shirt. She wasn't able to mind me, and she told me so. She said, "I can't take care of you, Mira, I just can't manage that."

Then she would talk about my father again, and about the damned Croats. Said they were all fascists.

I didn't like staying home; I kept escaping to the junkyard with the old auto tires. To the place that I'd found earlier, with the other children. They didn't exist for me anymore. Only the trees, the rusty iron everywhere, the sun shining through the leaves, the yellow grass.

I went alone, every day.

I craved this place. Other children, school, my parents—when I was there I didn't need any of them. I hid inside the biggest tire. No one saw me, no one knew I was there. I lived solo in my own world. And that's where it started, thinking up songs. I didn't play an instrument yet, and they weren't regular children's songs, just nonsense verses in the style of icky acky ticky tacky doggie woggie doo, but in Serbian.

Finally my mother forbade me to leave the apartment. At the time the Serbs had started their own army and were launching grenades at Zagreb. The Serbian boys who still lived in the city bought green uniforms and vanished. The word went out: This was a new war. You couldn't see it except when one of the young boys was brought back dead.

My mother locked me in, but I knew where she hid the key. I sneaked out.

One time when I came home a man was there. I knew him only from photos: Uncle Lou. He had long hair and looked like a rock musician. My mother explained to me that I needn't be afraid. Uncle Lou was taking me with him.

Lou had a minibus full of musical instruments and amplifiers. I cried as he drove away, and at some point I fell asleep. When I woke up, we were already in Germany.

Strange, what you forget, and what you don't.

I remember Uncle Lou pulling me out of the amp case and buying me a plastic cup of cocoa at an *Autobahn* rest stop in Bavaria. And me not wanting anything to eat.

Then I sat on the rear seat of the VW bus, next to this woman I didn't know, except she was Lou's girlfriend, and therefore my aunt. I looked out the window at a hilly, cold, white landscape.

I asked, "Is that snow?"

"What did you say?" the woman asked.

Uncle Lou explained to me that she didn't speak Serbian.

Even on arrow-straight *Autobahn* stretches I always got nauseous in his bus.

Maybe because the springs had so much give, it felt like being in a swing. Or maybe it was because on this first trip I was still full of the tranquilizers they'd stuffed into me.

Anyway, when the *Autobahn* got curvy, I started feeling pretty sick pretty fast.

I told the woman.

She didn't understand me.

I told Uncle Lou.

He said he'd pull over when he could.

Just then, it came pouring out of me. I bent forward and threw up on his neck.

He stopped on the side of the road, and the woman got out with me, but I was done.

As we came back to the bus, Uncle Lou was wiping the vomit from his neck. He laughed. "We're off to a good start," he said.

It wasn't always easy with him, but I know he saved my life. Not because he got me out of Croatia, for that war soon ended.

But because he got me away from everything else.

And because he gave me a guitar.

[TRACK 8]
THE STORY OF ZUCKA AND MELODY

1. The snow on the terrace melted as fast as it had fallen. Only a little dusted the flowerpots. In one of them Zucka put out his cigarette.

Through the bare trees he could see the Elbe, and behind it the container harbor. He sensed someone sidle up behind him. Not Rosa. He knew that she was in the kitchen, busy cooking her traditional anniversary banku. It was Melody in the doorway, and now stepping onto the terrace. And as always, when he and she were alone, a bittersweet longing overcame him.

He slipped his cell phone into his pants pocket.

"Who were you talking to?" Melody asked.

"Kralle."

"She's coming back?"

He turned around and nodded. "But I promised her, no more troublemaking."

"I didn't start anything."

"And no more discussions about who started what."

"But I have the right to defend myself when Rosa . . ." She stopped and took a breath. Then she drew close to Zucka and felt his jacket pocket, found a pack of cigarettes, and took one.

"Got a light?"

He nodded, searched through his pants pocket.

"I took good care of those fish," Melody said, as though to herself, and looked through the large window at the green-lit aquarium. She flitted her cigarette around, mimicking a little fish's motions. "*I* put one of those in there. I don't know which. But I bought it."

"And?"

"For three days it was hyperactive, darted around extra fast, then hit its head smack against the glass. After that it dozed and didn't move much, like the rest."

"They had it good when you were here," Zucka said.

Melody turned away from the aquarium and toward him. "Zucka . . . A lot went wrong between us. But . . ."

"But what?"

She looked him directly in the face, for the first time that day. Then she said, "If I still mean something to you . . ."

"Obviously. You . . ."

"What?"

Zucka shifted his weight from one leg to the other and murmured, "Obviously . . ."

Melody stepped away, through the open door to the apartment, and looked around. She asked, "Why was Rosa straightening up? What's she searching for? Did OK send the two of you?"

Zucka glanced toward the Elbe again.

"Do I really still mean something to you?"

"You'd changed," Zucka said.

"I was the same. And I needed you."

"Really?"

"Obviously, Zucka. And you know it."

He turned toward her, pressed his lips together.

She stooped and put out her cigarette in the same flower-pot he'd used. "When I had to leave here, I didn't get around to cleaning up," she said. "Left all sorts of things behind. Mostly unimportant. But—" She moved very close to him and said softly, "If you happen to find a tape, a very small one, you know, the kind that fits in a mini-cassette recorder . . ."

"Yes?"

"Could be . . . could be that something of mine is on it."

"Oh?"

"Obviously you're with Rosa now. But Mira . . . she got so much from 'Don't Wanna Be.' I'm not after her fame, really I'm not!"

Zucka rummaged in his pants pockets, then held out a small black cassette.

"You mean something like this?"

She looked from his face to his hand.

"Can I see?"

He teased, "Better not," and stuck the cassette back in his pocket.

Melody turned to the aquarium. She said, her voice low, "As soon as I have a contract I'll throw it away. Or Rosa can have it and frame the thing."

Zucka came close. "You know why I'm not giving it to you?"

Melody raised her shoulders.

"Because there's only me on it. And you won't be interested."

With that he handed her the tape. From another pocket he brought out the small black recorder and opened it. She put the cassette in. He pressed play.

Melody had counted on hearing her own voice. But it really was Zucka, clumsily rapping to a homemade background beat. The minirecorder made everything sound metallic and scratchy. This tape, she thought, had to be really old.

"Hey, cool." She took the recorder from him. He bit down on his lower lip while she kept listening a while.

"Today, of course, we'd use a digital recorder."

She hit stop. "Did you record that here?"

"You thought something else was on it?" he said.

"Yes, I thought . . ."

"I know."

"You remember?"

"Hey, that's one night I'll never forget," Zucka said.

"Never?"

"Never."

She smiled, looked toward the kitchen door again, and said, "You know, if I had that cassette . . . the one of me—"

"If I find it . . . ," Zucka said and swallowed. "You'll get it."

2. Zucka remembered: That night Melody had slept on the sofa, her coat pulled halfway over her legs. Her head tilted back, she snored softly.

Zucka had found it charming. He'd sat at the other end of the sofa, gazing at her. At some point he, too, had fallen asleep.

When he woke up again, she was sitting on the rug, writing in her notebook and humming to herself. Before her lay the small black recorder. That was in the time when Melo still dreamed of recording her own album of her own songs.

He watched for a while, then checked his cell phone. It was two thirty a.m. And then she picked up the recorder and sang something into it.

But what?

Yes, true, he'd never forget this night. But what was it she had sung?

Some pop song or other? Or was it really those lines, "I don't wanna be famous. I don't wanna be a superstar . . ." that later turned up in a song by Mira—a song that sold three hundred sixty-four thousand singles?

When Melody told Zucka that it was then she'd gotten the idea for the song, he did not contradict her. Later, when she mentioned it again, he still could not say.

Because memories change, change every time you remember them. You try to hold them fast, but . . . Every two lovers invent a past for themselves, even if they actually never become a couple. How you got to know each other, how you kissed the first time . . . And how you sat together, one summer night, in this giant apartment; how through the wide door to the terrace you heard the crickets chirping and the thuds and rattles from the container harbor; how Melo'd had an idea for a song and wrote a few lines; how she'd sung a refrain into the recorder, so as not to forget the tune. . . .

Zucka asked himself if that story had really begun that night—the story of the song that sold so very well, the story that ended with a young singer lying dead in an aquarium?

Or maybe earlier? He wondered . . . Maybe it began on the day he first met Melody.

That day when he mentioned his papa to her, and EOK Productions . . .

3. Four years ago, on "another gray Hamburg winter afternoon on the last day of the last year of the last decade of the last century of the second millennium," as Giorgio so eloquently put it.

A torn guitar string, an empty coffee can in the refrigerator—trivial, annoying things made Zucka and Giorgio give up on trying to mix a song. And they left the studio.

Melody, who was still Luisa then, stood in a bakery, drinking coffee. She'd put her loose-leaf binder of song lyrics on the counter, and was humming quietly.

Giorgio had wanted to go to the Italian place, have an espresso. But then, catching sight of her, he stopped in front of the bakery window.

"Nice view."

"Where?"

"Three degrees north-northeast." Giorgio pointed to Melody. "Let's go in."

"Go in?" asked Zucka. "And then?"

"Talk to her."

Giorgio pushed the door open with his guitar case. Zucka followed. They got coffee for themselves and stood a distance away.

Zucka was eighteen back then. And hoping to talk to this woman with the face of an African model was a whole other thing than coming on to a tenth-grade girl at a high school dance.

Yet the longer he stared at her, the more certain he grew that he must not leave this bakery without having talked to her.

He said, "We have to—"

"That's what I'm telling you," Giorgio said.

"We could ask for a cigarette and a light," Zucka suggested.

Giorgio slurped his coffee. "That one ranks first on the list of worst pickup lines."

"Didn't know."

"Asking for a light is okay. Let's."

Zucka searched through his pants pockets. "But we haven't got cigarettes."

"A light is cool. Cigarettes, shit."

After twenty minutes Zucka still stood there, his coffee finished. Giorgio had gone home long since. Melody was packing her shoulder bag. Zucka knew that he had to go over to her now and say something. Just then she came over to him.

He stared at her with glazed eyes. She stood before him, tall, slender, wearing a pale blue training suit never intended for training. And outfits like that weren't sold in supermarkets back then, only in select hip clothing stores in the Karo quarter.

Anyway, she smiled.

He couldn't get any words out.

She asked, "Do you have a light?"

Only then did he see the cigarette between her fingers.

"Nah," he said. "And no cigarette, either."

She rummaged in her bag, nudged a pack open, and offered him one.

Zucka took it, looked around. "I'll go get a light."

Finally, he was able to light her cigarette from his.

"Thanks." She puffed somewhat ineptly.

If at the time he could have seen more clearly, he'd have recognized that she was not a smoker, that somebody else's cigarette pack must have landed in her bag, that the only reason she'd taken one out was so she could ask this awkward, slovenly, dreamy young guy for a light.

Which she regretted right away. Because Zucka blew smoke directly in her face.

"I heard you sing," he said.

"That was just something for the school choir."

"It was nice," Zucka said. "I know a little about that. You could be a professional."

"You think so?"

He leaned his elbow on the table. "Want a coffee?"

"I just had one. And no time."

Zucka took a deep drag of his cigarette. "Where do you have to go?"

"Please understand. I don't have to go anywhere. It's just, I don't have time."

"You think I'm stupid."

"No, it's nothing to do with you. I don't have time. It got away from me. I lost it."

"You lost the time?"

"Yes."

"Hmm." Zucka pushed the ashtray closer to her. "But sometime . . . could we play music together?"

She put out the cigarette and looked around. "Yes, I'd like that, but . . . I think I . . ."

Zucka realized he was getting nowhere with this woman. And right then, without actually wanting to, he drew his papa into it.

"We've got a studio," he said. "You know Hot Butter? We produced them. And . . ."

4. And notice: Zucka said "we." "We produced them." Actually, he hadn't had much to do with it. Hadn't wanted to. Zucka hated his papa, because Papa made garbage for the charts and Zucka was a purist hip-hopper. He wanted to be, anyway.

It's funny how Zucka twice intervened in my life. Once, when he came on to Melody, and then a few years later, when he gave a party to which his papa came, and "discovered" me.

If Zucka hadn't conned Melody into the studio . . .

Then Melody wouldn't have gotten to know OK, and then Rosa wouldn't have gotten to know OK, and also I wouldn't have.

And I wouldn't have played this song at Zucka's party.

And OK wouldn't have told me, "Play it again."

And this song, which actually wasn't so important to me, would presumably never have been produced. "Don't Wanna Be Famous."

And later no one would have claimed that *she'd* gotten the idea for it.

If Zucka hadn't conned Melody into the studio . . .

But why, of all people, Melody? He'd never done anything like that before, or afterward, either.

He knew what made him interesting: his daddy.

Because, let's face it, Zucka wasn't that interesting.

Sorry, Zucka.

Woolen hats like in *South Park*, baggy jeans, and that ghetto attitude, as though he didn't have rich parents and wasn't raised in luxury.

And he liked to quote wise old proverbs, believed in numerology, and swore that 9/11 was predicted in the Bible. I mean, how can you take that stuff seriously from someone who's frying his brains on pot? And what did it really have to do with hip-hop?

I didn't understand that Zucka, like the rest of us, just needed to break out, get away somehow; that yes, he too had grown up in a ghetto. Not a ghetto of corrugated-iron shacks or housing projects, no. His ghetto featured one-family homes with gardens out front and aromatic candles in the foyer. And always good things to eat and nice big new TVs.

Here's what Zucka had in common with us: We'd all lived inside holding pens, containers we needed to escape from. And to escape, we had to leave our worlds, become homeless.

For Melody it was Rose Hill; for me, Zagreb and the housing project; for Kralle, Ribnitz with its 40 percent unemployment. And for Zucka, well, it was a cushy suburb, Poppenbüttel, and a proper, middle-class life. His parents were divorced, of course, because by the time a type like OK turns forty or so, he must have a new, young wife. Zucka grew up at his mama's, where he got dusted with gold powder daily. Mama didn't work, because OK paid her plenty of support. She sat at home all day with nothing else to do than see that her boy had everything he wanted. He got loads of stuff. Psychologically I guess this was prolongation of the oral stage—Zucka forever the infant at the breast. With Mama in total control. So maybe Rosa, our "mama," was the right one for him after all.

But back then it wasn't Rosa on Zucka's mind. It was Melody.

It was hip-hop.

It was breaking away from the ghetto of Poppenbüttel.

Zucka had pulled on a new identity like a costume—baggy

pants, ratty pom-pom hats, the homeless look—but with a
certain air that he thought made him look cool.

Well, sort of. Zucka had style, he wasn't sexy. Maybe
because of the religious stuff. Or acting pissed off about
everything all the time. That's okay, if you really are. But if
you're clueless, it's not.

Anyway, Zucka had a problem with women. He knew it too.

Which is why he conned Melody into the studio, to EOK
Productions. Showed her all the equipment, acted like he knew
his way around. Played the song he and Giorgio had been
fiddling with. And on that evening, she wrote down her cell
phone number for him. The evening of the last day of the last
century of the second millennium, December 31, 1999.

I remember Zucka appearing late that New Year's Eve.

We were celebrating in Kralle's new flat above the
Shanghai Hotel on the raunchy *Reeperbahn*—Kralle, Rosa,
Melody, Jackson, and me, Mira M.

There's an old German custom that we'd picked up: You
drip bits of melted lead into water, and tell fortunes by the
shapes they form. That's what we were doing. And Melody's
cell phone kept ringing. Zucka must have called her twenty
times. Till she finally told him where we were.

We'd all been urging her to.

"Melo, are you trying to hide this guy from us?"

Zucka—together with his buddy Giorgio—showed up
shortly after two.

And here begins a romantic love story, but one we have to

set aside for now. Because Kralle is back, in her transparent
plastic raincoat. She rings the doorbell. And Zucka ushers her
in like she'd never left to walk along the Elbe in the snow. I
have to watch and listen, because they'll certainly talk about
me again. . . .

[TRACK 9]
JANUARY 14, 2004:
PART THREE

1. But they didn't talk about me.

Instead, harmony reigned.

Kralle unpacked her famous lasagna again. "Without it, where would we be?" Rosa asked.

Zucka said, "I still remember the first time I tasted it."

"It's something you don't soon forget," Melody added, wrinkling her forehead.

"I'm not in a joking mood," said Kralle.

When Rosa disappeared into the kitchen to warm up the lasagna, Kralle turned to Zucka and asked, "And what did you bring?"

"Drinks, as usual," Melody answered for him. "Or were there some already here?"

Zucka shrugged evasively.

Rosa looked in from the kitchen door. "Leave my sweetie in peace. He doesn't have much money just now."

So then they sat together like every year. And it *was* like every year, a little.

On January 14, 2004.

Rosa came out of the kitchen with Kralle's lasagna and a bowl of banku.

In 1997 there were five of us. And we decided we'd have
an anniversary feast on every January 14 from then on. Later
Zucka came along. That made six. Now only four were left.

Jackson was missing, he'd gone back to Ghana.

And me.

And now it was more like a funeral feast.

That's what Rosa thought too.

"Your banku is first-class," Kralle said.

Rosa nodded. "Mama's recipe," she said, pointing her fat
fingers at herself.

Melody shuddered. "It tastes like bones and innards, that
dish."

"It's made of corn, it's healthy," Rosa said, heading for the
kitchen. "I'll fix dessert."

"There's dessert?" Zucka asked.

"Of course there is, my sweet."

Kralle said, "I'll come with you," and followed Rosa.

Zucka and Melody stayed behind. Melody at the aquarium,
Zucka leaning on the big table in the center of the room. They
looked at each other. Zucka thought of the millennium New
Year's when he'd met Rosa, Kralle, and the others. And after
the party, bringing Melody home. Thinking his heart would
burst when she kissed him good night, on the cheek...

[TRACK 10]
IN THE CONTAINER

1. So, while in that historic year 2000 nothing really happened between Zucka and Melody, things with me and Jackson were slowly heading downhill.

We'd met almost three years ago, and I wasn't fourteen anymore, nor Jackson fifteen.

I've skipped over this love story, simply because . . . well, because stories arise out of conflict.

Kralle explained this to me: Every story needs a conflict, because without conflict characters don't emerge, and . . . no characters, no story. With Jackson and me everything was too smooth, that was the catch. The gods won't watch forever, they don't like it when anyone's too happy. Especially when it's me.

Jackson . . . could kiss like a world champion.

Could listen for hours and then say something very smart.

He wrote romantic poems for me. But his German was pretty bad. . . .

The beautiful thing about love: You suddenly get everything. You're told that you're fantastic. That you're beautiful. That everything you do is wonderful. That you have a gorgeous nose, regardless of what the mirror tells you. You get to hear all those good things, and get looked at by a pair of eyes so honest, and so tender. Suddenly there's nothing you need to prove, you can be exactly as you are. And get loved for it.

We could sit together for hours, lie next to each other. I felt
his nearness; that was enough for me. He clearly liked it too.

And if you add good sex to all of this, it is the ultimate
addiction.

I slowly grasped what it must have taken, doing what he, and
Rosa, and Melo had done. I mean, when you're that young,
hiding out in a container because you sense that escaping
Africa is your only chance.

They'd huddled in total darkness. Darkness that eyes don't
get used to. Utter nothingness around them.

I knew the feeling—from when I was nine and woke up
shut inside a narrow case, in the baggage space of Uncle Lou's
bus. I couldn't see even my own body. Like being in a coffin,
buried alive. My heart was racing, strange things happening in
my head. Somehow I was sure that I looked dead, like people
in horror stories, that I was already buried deep down in the
earth. And I was terrified that any moment I'd stop breathing,
and be really dead.

Then the bus got going again. I heard the motor, felt the
bumpiness, and I remembered my mother's face when she
explained to me that I had to be smuggled into Germany,
and I'd be hidden, but that I could sleep and wouldn't be
afraid. Then the tranquilizers they'd fed me kicked in again. . . .

Jackson, Rosa, and Melo had no tranquilizers in them. They
didn't get to go back to sleep.

Jackson told me that when you're in such total blackness,

your head starts making pictures. He told me that his mind took him to where there was sunshine, bright daylight. "Inside your head, you can be everywhere," he said. "But the funny thing is, I was always just in one place: home. In front of the house where we lived. I could have been anywhere, even America, inside my head. But I was always back there, in Liberia, and it was always bright, and there was always plenty to eat and drink."

Jackson lay beside me on the mattress. Only the little light under the kettle was on. I could feel his breath when he told me this. "But then later, you stop picturing these places," he said. "We'd been without water for three days. I'd had a bad feeling when that man brought me to the harbor. A strange man, and I sensed right away that it wouldn't be good. And at some time you just know. You stop thinking about how you'll survive, all you think about is how you'll die. In the beginning, I'd imagined the container would open and I'd be in a strange place. Later I imagined the container opening and me lying dead, dried out like leather in the sun, and being carried out into the morning."

"And then?"

"Then I woke up. Here in Hamburg. And so you realize you do survive—if that's the word. But you don't, really."

For me Rosa, Melody, and Jackson had always been a unity. But it was sheer coincidence that they were in the same container on the same ship, came to the same city, and met the same people. Kralle, me. And Zucka. And OK.

When she already lived in the apartment, and I sometimes slept there, Melody would tell me about the crossing. And about her childhood. About Rose Hill. And the world map.

Melo and I—we were as different as two people could be. But there was something that connected us. The music, naturally. Singing. But there was more. Something that led to our stories intertwining. Melody becoming my fate, and I hers. Or something like that...

Anyway, I'd never have moved into OK's apartment if it hadn't been for Melody. And Melody wouldn't have moved out if there hadn't been me.

2. If you want to understand what happened with Mira, and why, one January morning in 2004, she lay bleeding in the giant aquarium—then you first must know what happened with Melody.

Melody, who first was called Luisa.

She grew up in Rose Hill, a small suburb on the road to Tema in south Ghana.

The difference between Luisa and the other children of Rose Hill was that she wasn't entirely black. Rather, she was light brown, the color of rich loam.

Melody's mother was as black as all the people in Rose Hill. But she wanted out. Her whole life long. And if she didn't get out, she'd see to it that her child could.

Melody's mother took a white man to have a baby with, so that the child would have a chance. That's what she said. "In vain," she always added. "You didn't make use of the chance," she said to Luisa. Because the child didn't turn out white enough.

Whenever Melody spotted a big, loose-limbed man with light hair and freckles, she thought he might be her father. Whom she never met.

Luisa's mother had bad luck. The white man took off before he knew she was even pregnant. And the child didn't look a lot like him. Was only light enough for the other children in Rose Hill to treat her as an outsider.

The kids of Rose Hill hung around outside all day. Luisa stood in the little store, in front of the world map that was fastened to the wall. At the top were ads for phone cards: Europe fifty cedi, America one hundred cedi.

While others played soccer or just ran around, she stood gazing at the map. And she saw the sea grow darker every day. Later she understood that it was because the dampness of the wall was gradually dissolving the paper. But when she was little she took it to mean that the whole world was slowly darkening.

One time as she stood watching, a spider crept from Africa to Spain. The lines of shipping routes were the spider's web.

And little ants ran around the equator. Sometimes an ant would stray off course into Luisa's land, the little yellow country where Rose Hill was.

"Don't dream," said her mother and pulled her away. Luisa's mother was always in a hurry. "If you want to live, you have to be awake."

And she added in a disappointed voice, "Once Rose Hill, always Rose Hill. Whoever grows up here doesn't get out." And it was true. Luisa didn't know anyone who'd gone away and hadn't soon come back.

Rose Hill consisted of corrugated iron, wooden planks, a small store. If you were older than ten, there was no school.

Once, when her mother had yanked her away, Luisa tore loose and ran back to the map. The mother grabbed Luisa by her braid, pulling her so hard that she fell on the street, then hit the girl with the shopping bags she carried. In the bags were cans of meat that struck Luisa's head, a big papaya that hit her on her back, a pineapple that cut her hand—and the bags tore open and everything fell on the street. The papaya burst in the dirt, and the mother cried.

One time Luisa saw a famous singer on TV who told everyone how she'd lifted herself out of poverty by singing.

That night Luisa decided that she would learn to sing. Of course she had no money for lessons, and there was no one in Rose Hill who could teach her. But she did everything the singer on TV had done: At the lake, washing clothes, Luisa ducked her head under for so long that her lungs almost burst. And when no one was watching, she put big stones on her belly to tauten her muscles. And spoke with pebbles in her mouth.

And she'd sit by the radio and sing along with all the songs.

+   +   +

Early one morning when she was fourteen, she boiled water, filled two large bottles, and slipped away from home. She came into Tema as it slowly grew light. Around her the traffic roared.

There was a newspaper with fashion photos, which almost all the women in Rose Hill bought. Luisa wanted to become a model for this paper.

She went to its office and was invited to a photo audition. They gave her fifteen thousand cedi and told her to come back the following week. Fifteen thousand cedi was twenty dollars. Luisa had earned more in one day than her mother earned in a month. She went back to Rose Hill.

She knew that in the capital, Accra, there was a school where singing was taught. She wanted to save money for the school. And she went every day to the big swimming pool because she could duck underwater better there than at the lake.

Evenings she stood at the harbor, where warm winds carried the smell of the sea. She saw the ships that brought old cars from Europe. Then, laden with containers, they sailed away again.

And she heard about the man who sold places.

[TRACK 11]
DON'T DREAM IT, BE IT

1. The good-looking psycho doc explained to me later that psychologists once advised people to live their dreams. But now the docs think just the opposite: that what they should explain to kids is that living a dream in a dreamworld makes no sense.

Maybe someone should have told Melo. A dream coming true can turn into something monstrous, a nightmare. But that happens later, of course. First it's the dream, and not just one dream, but many, giving birth to many more.

The beauty of Luisa's story is that something happened that we all crave: a dream came true. She struggled for it, and believed in it, till she started living like a princess in OK's giant apartment.

First though, Luisa had to become Melody.

2. I know how it is once you get to Zucka's papa. You feel like you're selling something you don't want to part with. Like when you're broke and go ahead and sell the favorite CDs from your collection to some sleazy secondhand store.

You're excited because you feel that something totally new is starting. That nothing in your life will be as it was.

And then when you sit facing him, you see that he's one of these people who can make dreams come true. Your dreams. And he can make you into the dream of thousands of other people.

You sense it. He has the power to create dreams—and destroy what he's created.

OK can be very nice, actually.

First there's an appointment on Sunday, when no one else is in the office . . . totally exclusive. The great producer has time for *you*. Is interested only in *you*. Even if some hotshot producer like Dieter Bohlen himself were to call, OK would say, "I'm in the middle of an important conversation. May I call you back?"

He won't grope you, or hit on you in any way. He's totally not like that. If he wants to do business with you, you needn't worry about that. For him there are only two kinds of women: One kind interests him sexually. The other kind, financially.

3. "My son has told me a lot about you, Luisa." OK sat on the edge of the desk and gave her the once-over.

"Yes?"

"Luisa . . ." He tilted his head and rubbed his chin. Looked up. "How about Melody?"

Zucka explained, "He means as a name. Your stage name."

She beamed. "Sounds fantastic."

"Good. So now you are Melody."

"Hey, Melody, how're you doing?" Zucka asked, smiling.

They sat in front of OK's desk in two black leather chairs. Zucka slumping, looking pale, because he could already tell that this was not going at all as he'd imagined.

Zucka's idea had been to produce something on his own with Melody. To experiment a bit. But now his papa took the initiative. And Melody, not at all interested in Zucka, sat very straight, paid strict attention, intent on OK's every word and move.

He came out from behind the desk, sat down in a third chair. "And what else do you do?" he asked.

"I'm still going to school."

"She's taking a course in finance," Zucka put in.

"That's good," OK said. "Very good."

"Everyone's against taxes," Melody said. "But taxes pay for everything: schools, kindergartens, hospitals, even theater. . . ."

"And the police." OK smiled, picked up a file of photos, and started riffling through them.

Zucka observed that Melody's eyes were glued to his papa, and he asked himself, *Does she even deserve my love? Is she going to let herself be eaten alive by EOK Productions?*

OK said, "Melody, you know, your youth is your biggest asset. Nowadays you have to reach the market at sixteen."

"I'm eighteen. . . ."

"You look younger. Let's say you're sixteen. Agreed?"

Melody nodded.

OK spread some photos out on the desk. They were of young singers dressed as go-go dancers.

"You have to make a clear distinction," he said. "The media image we construct has nothing to do with you. So then, you have two personalities. You think you can do this?"

He pointed to half-naked singers in the photos.

Zucka leaned back in his chair. He'd heard it often enough. His father always asked that.

"Why not?" said Melody.

OK said, "You have to be patient. You know, today . . . without a concept and marketing plan no one gets on the charts."

"I know," Melody murmured.

"We first have to build you up. We have to get to know you—the real you, find out if you can stand it. You have to understand, I've gone through all that with so many girls, invested two whole years, and by the time they're ready to start, they've changed their minds, they want proper careers, would really rather study law."

"I want to sing."

"It could happen that you have four shows in one night, at discos, clubs, music fests. . . ."

"I want to sing," Melody repeated.

Lots of people said that OK cared only about money. But Zucka, slumping in his chair, knew this wasn't quite so. Obviously his papa had an ice-cold feeling for who'd succeed. Because that was Rule Number One: OK's acts always made money. But Zucka knew his father also wanted to be *fabulous*. A fantastic guy. And when he had hot acts and produced a hit, then he was cool. That's what it was about.

And right then Zucka knew: He'd lost the girl he'd met in a bakery. She'd already started changing. Turning into someone else.

For Melody it was different, of course. She wasn't remembering the bakery. She remembered the days in the container, when they had no water, nothing to eat, and didn't know how long they could last.

And she'd sworn to herself: "If you get out of here, then you *will* make your dream come true. People will love you. And you'll be happy."

Now, in her mind, she told that girl, "I'm keeping my promise. You're going to sing and be really famous. And they'll love you!"

4. Luisa, now called Melody, would gladly have written her own songs, made up her own music, black, soulful R & B.

At the start of 2000, the music that clubs played was called techno, but in reality was fully synthesized pop: dull, computer-generated beats and simple tunes from children's songs endlessly repeated, sung in electronically distorted voices.

Two years earlier Zucka's papa had a dance act that made the charts: Hot Butter. He stuck Melody into that. Hot Butter consisted of two girl singers and one dancer, and toured major discos, industrial parties, tent festivals. Meantime the butter wasn't so hot anymore, had turned a bit rancid.

For a while OK really believed the group might land a hit again. They recorded an EP. And Melody took over as lead singer.

+   +   +

When the EP made the charts, OK asked Melody a question that changed everything. It sounded innocent enough. Would she take care of his aquarium?

That was the way he offered her the apartment. Rent free. Everything included: telephone, cable connection, pay TV, cleaning woman.

OK always only asked, "Would you mind looking after my fish?"

The apartment belonged to EOK Productions but was used only for large conferences and receptions, or for visits by prominent musicians who otherwise would have to be put up in a suite in the Hotel Atlantic. Since it was mostly empty, OK rewarded his current favorite with it.

This meant that Melody was now his Number One.

Zucka drove her there. When he opened the door and led her into the very large, bright room, Melody started to tremble.

She didn't think about the other young singer who'd taken care of the fish before her. She didn't ask what had become of her.

She saw the spaciousness, the polished stone floor that reflected light like a great mirror. She saw the broad expanse of windows, like a cinemascope screen, with a view of the Elbe; the luxurious white sofa; and the great aquarium, the only thing alive in this chilly ambiance.

She trembled with happiness. So she believed. Maybe she also trembled with fear.

[TRACK 12]
JANUARY 14, 2001

1. And so it happened that January 14, 2001 was the first time our anniversary feast took place in the big apartment with the splendid Elbe view. Melody had offered it.

I couldn't wait; I'd heard so much about the place from Rosa and Kralle, and of course from Melody herself. Rosa had something against it, but that was just envy talking, Kralle said. I agree that Rosa was envious. But still, she was right to feel uneasy.

From outside, if you were coming from the Elbchaussee, the building looked like a glass-and-metal box.

We went up the broad staircase, past enormous old trees—red beech and oak.

And finally stood before the great wooden entrance—to an entire apartment house, you'd have thought. But it led into a single space.

Jackson said, when he first saw it, "You can play soccer in here."

A great rush of space with reflecting stone tiles. And a window so wide, it took up almost an entire wall.

And behind it those trees, then the Elbe, the harbor, and then hills . . .

And lost somehow in this gigantic room, Melody.

In her training suit, sky blue.

Later Rosa told a story of a town house that once stood here and was torn down because nobody had wanted to move in. Supposedly, weird things had happened in it.

Total nonsense, I thought. Until I lived in this apartment myself. And started hearing the voices.

After a few weeks there, Melody seemed a bit spooked. But nobody paid much attention.

We all stood in the doorway, gaping. Zucka cried, "Ta-dah!"

Jackson took a few steps, looked around, and said, "It's true, you really could play soccer." Then he turned to Melody. "And you get to live here, just like that?"

She nodded.

Kralle crossed to the giant window, walked along it to the terrace: "Hey, look, the harbor. The containers." She opened the door and went out.

I joined her. "This is a whole other thing."

"Also not as much pigeon shit as on our little balcony," Kralle said, and ran back inside.

Jackson stopped at the aquarium, watched the fish circling slowly. "They're hardly moving," he said. "Stunned by an electric shock, do you think?"

I came over, hugged him from behind, and stuck my hand in the water. That speeded them up right away. They all came swimming, so trustingly. "Hey, you don't even know me," I said.

Zucka joined us. "See that eel? Papa fished it out of the Elbe. It crouches in its cave all day. But at night it comes out and grabs something to eat."

"Eels are disgusting," Kralle said.

"They have poison blood," said Zucka. "That's why no one messes with them."

"Don't the fish feel imprisoned?" I asked.

Zucka held a make-believe microphone over the water and asked in a nasal voice, "You guys comfortable in there?"

Now Melody stood next to us. "They don't give interviews, like really cool people."

"And you?" Kralle asked. "Do you give interviews now, or are you also too cool?"

"I'm also cool . . . but I give them if I get asked."

"And do you get asked?"

"It's starting slowly," Zucka said.

"Saturday I did three shows, Traxx, then Max, and then Bad Segeberg," Melody said. "Zucka's papa took care of everything. And I have no more problem getting approval for extending my visa."

Zucka groaned.

Melody pulled him to her. "OK is okay, even if you don't want to admit it."

"You already call him OK?" Rosa asked.

"It's actually like a real friendship," Melody said.

"What are you getting for three shows a night?" asked Rosa.

"Two hundred euros."

"For every night?" asked Jackson.

"I can live very well on that," said Melody.

"Two hundred every night?" Jackson repeated, as though he couldn't believe it.

"And you?" Melody asked, "Anything happening with you?"

"Nah," said Jackson. "Things are shitty...."

Silence for a moment. Zucka glanced at the table and asked, "When do we eat?"

No one answered. Kralle turned to Melody. "Do you think you'll get famous now?"

"I don't care about that pop-star shit," Rosa cut in. "I have no wish to be famous."

"I don't want to either," said Melody. "But if it should happen..."

"Me, I'd like to be famous," Kralle said.

"Right. But not for your lasagna," Melody said.

"As a writer," said Kralle.

"All you need is the right material," said Zucka.

"Everybody wants to reach their audience," Melody said. "Whoever denies that is lying, to himself or to others."

Rosa sat in the orange swivel chair in the middle of the room. "You know why they're called pop stars. Because of all the pills you have to pop to get to be one."

Melo leaned on the arm of her chair. "You know I'd never do that."

"You're no pop star either."

"Not yet," Kralle said.

I went to the window again. The view was really cool.

"From now on, we can meet here every year," Melody said. "No problem..."

Rosa said, "Yeah. If you're still living here next year..."

+   +   +

2. Jackson once said, "Here in Germany so many doors are open. You just have to pick one and go ahead. And then that's your life."

Endless possibilities. What you don't realize is that many doors close, fast. That opportunities get lost.

On that January 14 I went home with Jackson. We walked along the Elbe arm in arm to the fish market, then up to the *Reeperbahn* where I lived, at Kralle's.

If I'd known this was the last time I'd walk through those streets with Jackson, I'd have pulled him closer. And when we parted a few hours later, I wouldn't have given him only one kiss. I didn't know. But I already felt anxious, uneasy.

Like I said, I sensed at the start that it wouldn't last forever between us. What's strange is that when things got problematic, I didn't notice. Maybe because I didn't want to, or else because I thought he was right. I couldn't see that he'd let himself get hamstrung in a way that would be ruinous.

I read this in one of Kralle's clever books: To live means to say yes to life twenty-four times a day. You must always keep on going. Always get up again.

But how do you do it? Say yes all those times, when you don't really know who you are or why you're doing whatever? When you're falling into your own shit every hour and going around and around in circles, like a cat trying to catch its own tail?

To live means change. I was done with school and didn't know what I should start. But I changed. Moved when Kralle did, into the *Reeperbahn* flat. Found a night job working at a gaming arcade. That freed up my days. No more school, no more stress, lots of time to think about things. I got a whole new outlook on the world. And Kralle gave me these pseudo-psychology books about finding yourself, about spirituality. Not that I took it all in word for word. Still, it opened up lots of new questions. I started to be interested in Buddhism. It dawned on me that there was more to life than I'd suspected.

And Jackson changed too. At first I didn't want it to be so. He was still in eleventh grade.

Everything that went wrong in his life he now blamed on other people. And on Germany. It was Germany's fault that he hadn't finished school, and that he felt rotten. For months he talked only about that.

When he was really so cool! I don't mean just his looks. He was bright, he had such a good mind. He could talk about highly philosophical things in a way that put Kralle's psycho-books to shame. And you knew by his gestures and how his eyes glowed that those things really excited him.

But he talked less and less about them as time passed. And I didn't notice.

Until that night, after he saw Melody's apartment . . . that must have been the final straw for him. Of course. Rosa's place was the size of a closet, in Barmbek, but her own. Kralle and I had the *Reeperbahn* flat. And now Melody lived like a princess

in a palace—while Jackson was stuck in a twelve-square-meter
room in a shelter with just a cot, not a real bed, to sleep on.

We made it to Kralle's hole in the wall around half past one.

Besides her and me, two guys lived there who smoked pot
all day. It looked as you'd expect. So what? I put the kettle on,
we lay down on my mattress.

I thought, *We'll take a few sips, then we'll sleep.* Just lie there,
like little brother and little sister—not that I had anything
against sex.

But that night Jackson wanted to talk.

Or gripe and grumble, you might say.

As I've already mentioned, he took everything so personally.

"If you want to become a personality, you have to take
things personally," he said, in English.

Typical. He still only half spoke German. After four years.

Melody and Rosa spoke it fluently with accents so slight,
you almost couldn't tell that they weren't born here.

Jackson could communicate simple needs quite well in
German. But nothing more. Not that he'd communicated
much of anything lately. Except when he was on his loser jag,
then he went on and on.

That night he started telling me about some kid. In the
third person. At first I didn't catch on, or didn't want to, that
he was talking about himself.

In the dark I almost couldn't see his face. I only heard his
gentle but excited voice:

"Once there was a boy who lived in a rich land. . . ."

[TRACK 13]
JACKSON'S STORY

1. And this boy felt that he was getting smaller every day. He'd been content with the world and with himself, but here, in the rich land, he slowly lost his self-respect. Each day was like an exam, or a long class assignment testing his patience, his emotions, his principles. . . .

The teacher made life hard for him, for no particular reason. Teachers always have ways of keeping themselves entertained. They conduct experiments, like children watching how long it takes for the ant to slowly melt under a magnifying glass.

Then, too, he had to report to the immigration office weekly, never knowing if he'd be granted permission to stay in the rich land one week more.

At first the boy wanted to be like the others in his class. He tried to learn the language and to play their games. Soon enough he noticed that he didn't fit in. He knew that it wasn't the color of his skin, or anyway, not that alone. Because Rosa and Melody were doing well. Only he still had to report to the immigration office every week, and his teachers never gave him passes for that.

The other kids in the youth shelter all dealt drugs. They made piles of money. If you looked in their rooms, you saw stereo equipment, computers, lots of CDs. The boy didn't have those. Because he'd sworn to himself that he'd never deal drugs. He knew that dealing was a dead-end street. That someday, unavoidably, you'd get caught, get sent back to Africa.

But then he asked himself, why should only *he* stay honest? No one else was. Not the teachers, not the caseworker, not the students, not the others in the shelter. Nobody was honest.

And that was the reason he didn't fit in anywhere. Once he understood this, he started to enjoy that he was considered different. An outcast. He thought the others' funny cracks were stupid, because they were really about someone else who only superficially resembled him.

Yet the boy was stuck: Any misstep he might make could take him back. If a fight broke out at school, and students were called before the director, and if he was one of them, it could happen that he'd have to return to the land from which he came.

And he asked himself, *Why don't you deal, like the others?* He was smart enough to know that addicts existed regardless of whether he dealt or not. Tens of thousands of addicts in this big city used heroin daily. Somebody had to provide it.

Though the boy grasped that much, don't think he started dealing. He built a firewall around himself. A wall built of many protective shields. From inside this safety zone he saw things much more clearly: That life consists of pain. That when you live, somebody else feels pain. That when you eat, somebody else feels pain so that you *can* eat.

You can either deal heroin so that people can have something to deaden the pain, or you can do something to make the pain even greater—so much greater that everybody will notice what is going on. . . .

The next time the boy came to the immigration office, he was happy. He felt light. He laughed at the caseworker's dumb jokes. Life was beautiful. And no one suspected that he had two packets of explosives and fuses in his pocket. Or that earlier he'd deposited five packets in trash cans around school. Or that he'd strapped some on himself.

No one had a clue. He was waiting for the perfect . . .

2. "Jackson, wait!" I said. But he didn't listen. And went on about himself in the third person. About this boy who had no name.

Actually, I could relate. I'd been an outsider long enough. But not a bomber. Now I argued, "Listen, those other kids don't mean it like that. They're just frustrated themselves. . . ."

"You think so?" he asked. "And why should I suffer their frustration?"

I sat up. "Come on. Have a little tea."

He stood, started putting on his clothes. "Your tea won't make things any better."

He said it in German.

I suddenly stopped wanting to understand him. I'd listened long enough. I'd listened to him for weeks and weeks, telling me and everyone how shitty everything was here.

I sat there with the teapot in my hand. And thought: *If that's how it is, then leave.*

And he left. Stooped down quickly, kissed me on the cheek.

I thought, *Okay*. But it wasn't. I never really got over that it was over.

Next day he went to the immigration office for his regular appointment. With no explosives strapped on. And he had not hidden any in school. He did bring something with him, though. A letter to his caseworker, asking for a more extended permission to stay. He didn't want to keep coming to the office every Monday, spending hours waiting there, just to get the official stamp. He told his caseworker that he wouldn't be showing up the following week.

He didn't hide. He kept going to school. Ten days later they came for him. The counselors at the shelter tried to reason with him. But Jackson wasn't willing to renew his application.

For six weeks he was in the deportation queue, in the cellar of the interrogation prison Holstenglacis. Then a border patrolman took him, handcuffed, to Berlin.

Before they got on the train he was allowed to make one phone call.

Kralle borrowed a car and we drove to Berlin, to the airport. That's where I saw him for the last time, in a small cage with only enough room for a wooden bench.

He was glad we came. I was off him, done with him. I did, and didn't, understand him. But I cried when he raised his eyebrow in that special way and smiled at me.

There was nothing we could do for him. He didn't want to stay here anymore.

Since he was quiet and well behaved, they hadn't shot him full of sedatives or put tape over his mouth.

The plane took off punctually at ten.

Two months later a letter came from Tema. "Everything is okay," he wrote, "I'm planning to open a video theater." And he ended with:

"My whole being longs for you."

After I read this letter, I sat in my room in the *Reeperbahn* flat. I took up my guitar and played a song that I'd written four years ago, on a Sunday afternoon in the *Bauwagenplatz*.

> *You won't understand me*
> *Not in a thousand years.*

I'd sat by the fire pit. And a fifteen-year-old boy, who'd just come to Germany in a container, listened to me, watched me with his dark eyes.

> *You lie beside me every night*
> *But I don't feel you . . .*
> *You give everything you've got*
> *But I don't want it.*

When I'd played the song three times I leaned the guitar against the shelf by my bed. And I knew that it was time for me to find myself a band. And really make music.

[TRACK 14]
DON'T WANNA BE FAMOUS

1. When Melody was still called Luisa, and even before she started training the muscles in her lungs and abdomen, when she'd spent hours in front of the world map, she sometimes trekked into town with other children—on foot, two hours down the dusty road, but that didn't matter. Because in town, right next to the sea, there was a big park, with palm trees and flowers and a green meadow.

At the edge of the meadow there were stands where you could buy different kinds of eyeglass frames and lenses. There was also a stand where you could buy balloons in all colors.

Melody often looked at these balloons, and she knew they had a gas inside them that was lighter than air, and that's how come they could fly. But they didn't fly away, because the balloon seller had tied them fast.

One time Melody watched a girl point to a balloon, a girl in a bright dress with red and green flowers on it. Melody knew that girl was rich. A man wearing a European suit bought the balloon for her.

"I want to let it fly!" the girl called out. She let it go and followed with her eyes as it quickly rose into the sky. And disappeared.

Melody watched and grew frightened. She worried that

the girl would be very sorry she'd let the balloon fly away.

But the girl wasn't sorry. And the man bought her another one. She called out again, "I want to let it fly," and let it go.

The man gave the balloon seller a coin and chose a third balloon. The girl took it, came over to Melody, and held it out to her. "Here. You let it fly," she said.

Melody was thrilled. She gazed at the balloon.

"Let it fly," the girl in the flowered dress said again.

"No," said Melody, and held on tight to the balloon.

She held it tight all the way back to Rose Hill. The journey seemed a lot shorter with the balloon in her hand. In the small room where she slept, she let the balloon fly to the ceiling. There it stayed, and she looked at it all evening. She looked at it every day. After a week it darkened, shrank, and soon fell down, a crumpled little sack.

2. She often thought about that at four in the morning, lying in the big apartment, unable to sleep. About the balloon that had stuck to the ceiling until it fell down, emptied out and slack, back in Rose Hill, a suburb of Tema, when she was still Luisa.

Now, as Melody alias Melo and then Mel'O, she kept touring village discos. The name Melody hadn't made the breakthrough, though, and OK decided to rename her Mel'O and let her be a solo act. They recorded another EP that nobody bought. It was partly the marketing strategy's fault, OK explained. But actually he was already doing damage control.

Melody started writing her own songs, dreamed of an album with no techno on it, only soulful ballads. But OK made her keep on touring discos—for which she now got paid next to nothing because she had to work off the marketing costs of the EP that flopped.

Birds already twittered and the sun was rising over the harbor cranes when she came home after a night of doing three or four shows surrounded by dancing people all pumped up on pills. And she'd run up and down in the big apartment, exhausted and stressed out, watching her distorted figure reflected in the gleaming floor tiles.

When she'd moved in, she loved to stand on the terrace with the view over the river, the glittering harbor, the containers. It was as though she stood by the sea in Rose Hill. She thought then of the little girl who'd dreamed in front of the world map. And sometimes she thought of the balloon that she had not let go. She felt the salty breeze and believed she could fly. . . .

Now, a year and a half later, standing on the terrace she saw nothing, just grayness before her eyes. She heard nothing but the amplifiers' high-pitched buzz still lingering in her ears, and then one night, the murmur of . . .

3. . . . the voices. She told me about them one night, late—no, early, it was already morning. . . .

Whenever I'd had it with the *Reeperbahn* scene, I'd go and sleep in her cool apartment. Plenty of room. And I'd wake up around five in the morning when she got home and started pacing around to make herself tired. Sometimes she'd talk, nonstop. About the songs she was writing—which, frankly, wanted a delete key in my opinion; just a long sequence of clichés. I didn't say this to her. I could see she was in trouble. More and more so.

Once I woke up about seven, badly needing to pee, and she was standing in the middle of the room in her skintight, sexy stage costume, eyes shifting right and left, looking frantic. When I got back from the toilet, she still stood there like that. Like she was listening.

"What's up?" I asked.

"Don't you hear it?"

I said, "No, what?"

"Those voices."

I laughed and asked her in a joking way, "Are you going nuts now? Should I call a doctor?"

She shook her head. "No, something's here. Really."

Suddenly she leaned forward, reached into her pocketbook, took out her cell phone—and the voices were louder, I heard them too. She must have checked her voice mail and forgotten to click off, because her messages kept playing.

We both laughed.

But the subject was not closed.

Melody kept glancing around with that same panicky look on her face.

She really did hear voices. Not just on her cell.

One morning she sat with me on the white sofa, not

looking around in that panicky way. Instead she held her hands over her ears.

She said, "Soon I'll have to go to a psych clinic, maybe Ochsenzoll."

"Well, you'll have your own nice room."

"And free clothes."

She jumped up, went to the stereo, switched the radio on, and turned the volume up. She stood there a while, empty-eyed. Then she turned the volume higher—some teen song. They're all the same. She turned it even louder, nodded, and sat back down on the white sofa.

"And now?" I roared.

"It's better now."

"How about lying down, going to sleep?" I asked.

She shook her head. "Lying down? That's the worst."

"Maybe a sleeping pill?"

"That makes them louder." She sat up straight. "I know what a pill does after the kind of night I've had. At eleven we were in Buxtehude, at one in Bad Schwartau, at three in Kiel. . . . Tomorrow'll be better."

"You have to take care of yourself," I said.

"Can't be done."

"Those voices," I asked, "what do they say?"

Melody stood up, went out on the terrace.

She stood there in the rising morning mist and smoked a cigarette.

I went to her. The air was clear and cool.

+   +   +

I never found out what the voices were saying in Melody's head. But later I thought it wasn't so crazy, her insisting that they came from the apartment. Maybe she was right: They lived in this large, cool building in which nobody else really lived.

Leaning against the terrace door, smoking her cigarette, Melody turned to me and said, "You know about the town house that was here before? It stayed empty for a long time because ghosts lived here, supposedly."

"You shouldn't believe all that crap Rosa tells you."

She leaned her head on the silver metal door frame.

"Has it gotten worse recently?"

"Not worse," she said. "But louder. A few nights ago I tried sticking my head underwater, thought maybe that would help."

I stayed with her till she fell asleep on the big white sofa, still in her stage costume, breathing unevenly. I covered her with her woolen coat. Later, and that afternoon, I tried calling her, but there was no answer. The next weeks I didn't see her. I kept on calling, left messages on her machine. She didn't call me back.

One day Rosa said that all her shows had been canceled. That Melody was ill. No one knew anything more, except OK, of course. And he said nothing, just that she was getting better, and that the best thing now was to leave her in peace.

Zucka had to have known something, but no one really talked about it. We all assumed she'd had a breakdown and was in some psychiatric clinic.

Anyway, she didn't come to Zucka's birthday. A party for one hundred of his closest friends.

For me the beginning of the end.

CD 2: THE RISE AND FALL OF MIRA M.

[TRACK 1]
ZUCKA'S PARTY

1.

I don't wanna be famous
I don't wanna be who you are
I don't wanna be a trademark
I don't wanna be a wannabe superstar

I wanna be infamous, incapable, unfaceable, untraceable

So gimme just some place in time
And gimme some sweet bitter rhyme
And let me be forever mine
Commit my own crime
In my own time

Bitte bitte gib mir Liebe gib mir Sinn und Zweck
Gib mir Hass und Kraft für meinen Weg
Ob ich ihn gehe get dich einen Dreck an
Ich bin mein eigner Zweck
Auf meinem eignen Weg

I don't wanna be famous
I don't wanna be who you are
I don't wanna be a trademark
I don't wanna be a wannabe superstar.

2. In the winter of 2001 Zucka turned twenty, and his papa let him celebrate his birthday at a disco he owned a share in. A cool disco right on the *Reeperbahn*, with two dance floors, bars, and a chill-out room.

Zucka invited over a hundred people, and what with free drinks and all, a whole lot more than a hundred came. Zucka marveled at how many friends he had. He was particularly proud of the show program. It featured Zucka himself, rapping with a few pals, then Rosa and Kralle dancing like crazy go-go girls. And then, quite late, or rather, early in the morning, Mira playing a few songs with her new band, the Spiders.

This part wasn't really planned, Mira just did it because she hadn't brought a birthday present. Mira M. and the Spiders from Venus:

Giorgio on bass, already a professional studio musician, even for EOK Productions. He was calm and capable, maybe a little uptight. Ideal bassist, Mira thought.

Carlo on keyboards. He was born and raised in Hamburg, was not half-Italian like Giorgio. His real name was Karl. But they'd decided that all band members should have Italian-sounding names.

And Hannes on drums, not renamed yet, because he refused to be called Gianni. He was a perfect rhythm machine, blissfully smiling, providing the beat. "Maybe the only really talented musician in our band," Mira said of him, which Giorgio politely disputed.

Mira's finale at Zucka's party was new, not among the

songs she and the Spiders had been rehearsing and had made a demo of. She'd gotten the idea for it after she'd tried to present her material to OK. The song was called "Don't Wanna Be Famous." Playing it now, she goofed up every third chord change and garbled some lyrics that she didn't know by heart yet.

It was kind of a punk rock number with knife-sharp guitar riffs and merciless bass accompaniment. The melody was a bit too beautiful and soft for this hard sound, especially with three voices singing the refrain, but Mira had wanted exactly that mix, and it worked really well. Hard pop rock is what it really was.

As chance would have it, Zucka's papa came in just at the moment Mira switched on her amp and struck a distorted chord on her guitar. No, it was *not* by chance, Zucka said later, because his papa never did what people asked him to. And Zucka had begged him, Please *do not* appear at the party. . . .

When the last chord had been played and the crowd roared, cheering, there stood OK, quietly. But when Mira announced that this was the last song, and a special gift for Zucka, OK grabbed the DJ's mike and asked, "Won't you please play it again?"

Mira and many others looked in his direction. No one said a word. You could tell by Mira's expression that she disliked this overweight man with the perma-tan face.

OK dismissed her look with a smile. He could be charming

when he wanted. And he very courteously repeated, "Won't you please play it again?"

"Again?" Mira asked.

"Again!" roared the entire party.

She switched her amp back on and hammered out the intro on the strings.

This time everything went better—she only goofed once, at the transition to the bridge, and she got all the lyrics right.

Zucka's papa watched attentively. And when the DJ went back to dance music, OK slipped into a side room. There he poured himself a vodka. And sent somebody to bring her to him.

One of Mira's songs contained these lines:

I don't wanna want a thing
Even now when everyone's supposed to want something.

And she meant it.

She had qualms about OK. She'd seen what had happened with Melody. And a few weeks before Zucka's big party she'd met with him. To play him the demo she and Giorgio and the others had made.

It was Rosa's idea. "You don't make enough of yourself," Rosa kept saying. "You should go to him with your songs."

And OK had listened to the whole CD, seven selections, including lengthy organ solos by Carlo.

When it was over, he'd leaned back and explained why

one should pick only the strongest titles for a demo. "Because we music bigwigs don't have too much time," he said.

"Fine, but how do you like the material?" Giorgio asked.

OK stared ahead inscrutably.

"Oh well," he said after a while.

"That's all?" Mira asked.

OK didn't answer.

She stood up, packed her stuff, took the demo CD, stuck it in her shoulder bag. Giorgio and the boys just watched her. She motioned toward the door.

And . . .

3. . . . and now three of us sat facing him again, this time in the side room of the disco, while in the main room Zucka's party slowly ground to an end.

"What's up?" I asked.

"Want something to drink?" OK asked. Not waiting for an answer, he poured vodka into the water glass in front of me.

"Not so much," I said.

Giorgio and Carlo got vodka too. Hannes was still busy packing up his sticks and drums.

OK took a swallow from his own glass and said that this song "had real potential."

"A few weeks ago you told me that as a singer I won't amount to much," I reminded him.

"I did?"

"You did," said Giorgio from his perch on a gin carton.

"Oh well," said OK. "First of all, *prost!*"

"*Prost.*" We clinked glasses.

I was still pissed off. This guy had heard our recordings and jabbered on about how many new bands there were, how many new demo CDs, how not every hopeful kid can make it. We'd obviously only worked a few days on those songs, but now—out of the blue—he made me feel like some misunderstood genius.

He went on, "I can't promise you'll make it big, but that song of yours has it all: fantastic hook line, lovely melody . . ."

If there was one thing OK had an instinct for, it was sensing what it is that makes songs stick. He knew about that part of the brain, the prefrontal cortex. Certain songs get caught in it and stay there, can't be budged. Thanks to "hook lines." They're called that because they're like a hook swallowed by a fish, and it digs itself into the fish's innards.

With fishhooks you pull fish out of the water, and with hook lines you pull money out of CD buyers' pockets.

But OK did not explain all that to me at four in the morning on Zucka's birthday.

Not till the next day did he explain it, in his chic office in what, appropriately, had once been a slaughterhouse.

I sat there, still slightly hung over from Zucka's party, and had to listen to the whole rigmarole we already knew. Because Melody had heard it too.

That my youth was my greatest asset. That it was no problem to claim I was only sixteen. Although I was almost nineteen and had been in Hamburg almost five years.

"I feel like I'm sixty," I said, massaging my neck.

"You can't know what sixty feels like." OK sighed and quickly added, "I'm not there yet." Then he explained that I would be given a second personality. It wouldn't affect me personally. It would just be for the media. And first I'd have to be built up.

"I don't need anyone building me up," I said.

"I didn't mean it like that," OK said. "It's just that nobody makes the charts nowadays without a marketing plan. No matter how good you may be."

We met often during the following days.

OK had a problem with mixing English lines into some of my German songs, and vice versa. "Doesn't work," he told me. "It's hard to sell English-language pop songs played by German bands."

"But you have dance acts that sing in English," I said.

"That's something altogether different. Quite another market. It works in other ways."

I'm glad I didn't listen to him. Didn't make the same mistake that Melody made.

It's true, recording companies don't like a mix of English and German lyrics. Because the radio people don't like it. Doesn't fit into their pigeonholes, since it's neither pop rock nor German rock.

I never really thought about this, just did it because that's how the songs come to me. And suddenly everyone found it fantastic. Especially the same OK who'd explained that it never works.

+   +   +

We recorded "Don't Wanna Be Famous" in the studio with
the best sound engineers in the city. We'd done our seven-
song demo in just a couple of days; on this single we worked
for one entire week—till everyone was really satisfied. We
chose two more songs to record: "Hey You" and—this
pleased me especially—"Not in a Thousand Years." My
remembering-Jackson song. Even if it was really too slow and
schmaltzy and therefore, according to OK, "did not fit the
concept." We brought a real string quartet into the studio,
with violins, viola, and cello.

I wept when we mixed that song.

A few weeks later the EP came out.

And the craziness began.

[TRACK 2]
THE GREAT ROCK 'N' ROLL SWINDLE

1. At first it was all Chinese to me. All initials: There was the A&R—the artists and repertoire manager, in my case OK. Then the PM, who planned the marketing. And there was the Act (a singer, either gender, and a band).

To be an Act, you first have to have a deal, which means some producer has you under contract and pays you royalties on CD sales. Although most of the money comes from GEMA (the German Society for Musical Performing and Mechanical Reproduction Rights), not from the producer.

You can have a deal with a major label or an indie. There are only five major labels, big music factories. Warner, Sony, and like that. All the rest are indies, independents, even though these can be pretty big too.

I slowly found my way around in that world.

Luckily, Rosa made me realize right from the start that I needed a lawyer. I took Melody's story to heart and followed Rosa's advice. The lawyer was still working out the contract, or rather a sort of pre-contract, but there already was a marketing concept. I looked at it. Zucka tried to explain it to me but soon gave up.

That's when I first realized that what Zucka really did was

odd jobs for OK—like making tour arrangements. I wondered how he could stand it, feeling as he did about his papa. Well, he was young, he needed the money, and besides, it allowed him to be in the studio, fool around with computerized beats, and hang out with the hip-hop acts.

Meantime Rosa had started working there too and had become OK's assistant. She showed me the video storyboard he'd ordered.

It was supposed to be just a little fun film: Mira M. and the Spiders in scanty swimsuits, lazing around, slurping cocktails. And not even in the Caribbean, but on the North Sea island of Sylt.

I had my own ideas. I wanted it to be about a little girl smuggled across the border in a Marshall amplifier case. But first thing, straight off, there was the photo shoot. I nearly flipped out when I saw the takes. I looked like Ziggy Stardust 2002: blue-black hair, blue metallic eyelids, pale white face, glittery outfit, flared pants. Lots of sex, drugs, and rock 'n' roll.

From then on, things moved faster and faster. Before the CD was even ready, the first title got distributed to radio people. OK had explained to me that 90 percent of all singles flop, get nowhere near the top one hundred. So I was proud as anything when I happened to turn the radio on and suddenly my song was playing. Although they cut it off in the middle and ran a traffic report.

I stayed tuned to that station all day long but didn't hear the song again. Probably it came on when I was in the shower.

Then we did something pretty horrible: We toured through

half of Germany, doing promo gigs for media and sales types.
I gave my first interviews.

Music needs heroes, OK explained to me. And heroes need
an image. Well, I'd proposed this story for the video: Marshall
amp case, escape to Germany. First OK found it "far too
complicated," and "too negative." But then he changed his mind
overnight and decided to build everything on it. That's how he is.

They made up this image for me: Mira M., totally
independent, doesn't give a shit about the whole pop
music business. And then the story of the "Princess out of
Nothingness."

Yes, I'd proposed it myself. Because heroes need to have
been through some kind of ordeal. That gives them street
credibility, shows that they're trustworthy, OK explained. You
have to have a story, a fairy tale to enchant people with.

For me it was the story of Cinderella from Yugoland . . .
with a troubled childhood.

This story began in what's called the cold time, when a
war was fought in the middle of Europe. . . . When Serbs and
Croats, who for decades had lived together peacefully, all of a
sudden started shooting one another. Back then a little girl got
sedated with sleeping pills and stuck into a guitar amp case.
Not to abduct her. But to get her away from the horrible war
and bring her to the rich, happy land to the north.

If only I hadn't told OK!

But I absolutely wanted this video, featuring this scene:
the little girl creeping into the amp case, coming out as

Mira M., supercool in her glittery suit, and with her electric guitar. And like that . . .

2. So one day I sat in this upholstered swivel chair facing *Pop Tonight*'s sluttish interviewer and answering questions like, "How did you feel, all alone in a little box?"

"It was a Marshall amplifier case," I told her.

There I was, telling it on TV to umpty-thousand viewers: My father got arrested. By the secret police. My mother was suicidal. And my uncle . . . Uncle Lou saved my life, so to speak.

When you tell your story like that, and your face is on umpty-thousand TV screens, like all those other superstars telling how their child died, or their dog, and like ordinary people who, at two o'clock in the afternoon, talk about their sexual preferences—then you notice that something is changing inside you. I mean, you notice it if you're paying close attention. It's also possible to tell yourself that this is perfectly okay, just part of promotion, blah blah blah.

And, in fact, lots of teenagers, especially those not born here in Germany, related to my story, found it quite appealing.

I also gave real interviews. Talked to music journalists. One of those was pretty well known, worked for a paper that was somehow important. And he wrote—I remember the sentence: "Mira M. has gifted us with the most fantastic German pop single of recent years." Yes, really, "gifted us" is how he put it. Like for Christmas. And here's something else he wrote: "The Spiders are the coolest German rock band since Tocotronic."

Tocotronic! Jan, my hero! A few years back I'd decided to

marry him when I turned thirty. If he was still good-looking then. How many times had I listened to their music?!

Now I had it in writing: We were just as fantastic!

A week later we made it into the Media Control Charts waiting list. And then came the critical moment: The playlist meeting at MTV.

OK had explained to me that the decisive thing for a new band is to get into the MTV or the VIVA rotation. That's why he wanted to make a beach film. A little beach film. With lots of flesh.

Here's the thing: All big stations and channels, radio and TV, don't just play whatever they happen to find cool today. They have these so-called playlists. At MTV there's a Heavy List—those titles get played up to fifty times a week. And titles on the Hot List, twenty-five times a week. Then there's the Breakout List—titles not on the charts yet, but played just the same. What those titles are gets decided in weekly meetings. Also which three or four of the more than seventy new music videos will make it. Competition is pretty intense, especially if a new Madonna video has just come out.

OK had already invested not just the recording company's money but quite a lot of his own in our project. And VIVA had already rejected us.

Then came the playlist meeting at MTV. And we got into the rotation. Suddenly "Don't Wanna Be Famous" was on the air, three, maybe four times a day. The following week we reached the charts, fifty-fourth place right away.

That was a huge leap.

What Melody had not achieved in two years happened for us in just weeks, happened to me, Mira, the drab little mouse who'd always been in the background and who really only wanted to live quietly with some nice guy, and later maybe have a little house in the country and a couple of sweet children. . . .

"Famous" was a pretty cool song. But there were other reasons why it became a hit. It got us onto those cheesy open-audition shows in which performers act like idiots, and millions of teens lap it up. But of course there were other people—lots!—who thought those shows were stupid. OK was wise to them. He knew that whatever else they thought, they'd think "Don't Wanna Be Famous" was cool and would go out and buy it.

I don't wanna be a wannabe superstar!

And what happened was, we climbed into the top twenty, and then into the top ten, and then . . .

We almost made it to number one.

Meantime the next single had already come out, and it climbed too. "Not in a Thousand Years"—such a beautiful song, if I do say so myself.

So then OK asked, Would I take care of his aquarium in his giant, cool apartment on the Elbchaussee? All-inclusive, rent free.

I asked, "What about Melody?"

"Didn't she move out already?" he asked. "She wants to go to Berlin. Not interested in fishies anymore."

I hadn't seen Melody in weeks. If I'd bothered to think about this seriously . . .

But I didn't.

3. Sometimes, after everybody, even Giorgio, had left the studio, I'd sit all alone, strumming the guitar . . . till the chords I'd just played lapped like waves on the beach, into my brain and out again. . . .

And my gaze would grow unfocused, getting lost. . . .

Then suddenly a memory in black and white would come to me. A picture from before. A picture not of me, or other people, but of a place.

And one of these pictures was of my grandma's living room. The old, light brown matched armchairs and couch, the crowded knickknack shelves, and the view out the window: old people sitting downstairs on garden chairs, smoking and watching the children play.

Before, when Serbs and Croats were still talking to each other, Oma used to sit with them. Now she stayed in her apartment. And I didn't play with the other children in the building, because they peed in the elevator and did things like that.

So I, too, sat in the small apartment. While Oma puttered in the kitchen, I'd study the butterflies. My grandpa collected them when he was still alive—after he got his pension, and before he started dying, as my grandma put it.

The strange thing was, I used to think butterflies were pretty boring, even creepy. They looked sort of like overgrown ants with misshapen heads. But butterflies have wings. And those wings I liked.

I would stand for hours in front of his butterfly cases. I wasn't allowed to open them. And I didn't want to. I would just gaze at the colors and patterns. Butterfly wings are covered with very fine little scales, which I could see when I put my eye right near the glass.

Their feet are jointed, divided into three parts.

Their mouths are these weird sucking trunks—like those of miniature elephants.

I had learned all the butterfly species:

Peacock.

Glass wing.

Blue Admiral.

And I also knew that butterflies, like a few other insect species, went through a complete metamorphosis: from egg to larva, then pupa, and finally imago.

So there I'd stand, in my grandma's living room. The warm summer air of Zagreb drifted in through the open window. I listened to classical music on the radio and dreamed up stories about butterflies, their fairy-tale adventures. The butterflies traveled to America, flew through the universe, suffered tragic love affairs. . . .

My favorite butterfly was not one of those exciting, multicolored ones Opa had bought or traded others for. Not a peacock or glasswing. My favorite was a simple yellow lemon butterfly.

He was in every story I invented. The bigger, stronger

butterflies made fun of him and beat him up, but he always
triumphed in the end.

My grandpa once told me how he'd caught it. It was many
years before when he still lived in Vojvodina. Maybe that's why
I loved that butterfly so much.

Males have the yellow wings, females have whitish
ones. Their habitat is all of central Europe. Their life span is
three days. In summer, when butterflies danced in the air as
high up as the seventh floor, I'd stand on the balcony and hold
my hands out in the wind, and sometimes a lemon butterfly
would come winging and lightly graze my skin.

I never tried to touch it, because I knew that if you do, the
butterfly must die.

Once when Oma sat out on the balcony, and I was inside
gazing at those butterfly cases, something magical happened:

I had undone the lock, raised the lid of one case, and
carefully pulled out the pin that held the lemon butterfly. I laid
him in the palm of my hand. I just wanted to look at him. But
suddenly I felt something—a tickling sensation, as though the
butterfly's body were moving ever so softly, lightly. And then I
felt it distinctly: The thin little legs were moving.

I saw him slowly crane upward. The lemon butterfly,
imprisoned under a glass lid for who knew how many years,
stretched his legs. His wings twitched, very slowly at first,
like a machine long out of use, then faster. I heard a rushing
sound. And up he fluttered.

I sat there astounded, my hand still open, and could not
stir, could not utter a sound, just stared, watching the yellow

butterfly dance through the living room and to the balcony door. When he flew out, I leaped up, calling, "Oma, Oma, the butterfly!"

I ran after him and saw him sit on the balcony railing for a moment, then fly off.

And I called out, "The lemon butterfly!"

Oma just looked at me and said, "Yes, a lemon butterfly."

Later, when she discovered that one of Opa's specimens was missing, she got angry and forbade me ever again to play with the collection.

I looked at it another time, years later, after Oma's funeral. I was helping my mother clean out the apartment, and there it was, the empty place where the lemon butterfly had been. If you looked closely, you could still see the yellow outline he had left behind.

4. I thought of that butterfly on the stormy autumn day when, lugging two tote bags crammed full of my stuff, I climbed up the broad steps from the Elbchaussee to OK's apartment.

It was that kind of moment.

I'd always felt so certain that I wouldn't be lucky and that no one would care about me. And here I was, little Mira with her chewed-off fingernails, turned into a butterfly with metallic blue eyelids and a lilac mouth! Hair orange at the moment, but that would soon change.

I hadn't been to the apartment since I'd lost touch with Melody. It was a little scary seeing it again.

Rosa had told me that Melody planned to move to Berlin,

or had gone there already. And that she hadn't been feeling too well lately.

Halfway up the steps I stopped, looked up at ragged clouds crossing the sky, and at the trees, and the maple leaves dancing—like butterflies in the air.

I felt as though a long, long journey was ending. As though my wandering lay behind me. As though I was arriving at the place where I'd felt safe, at home, where things would be just right. As though I was returning to the junkyard with the great big tire. To the place where things were just exactly right. Although of course OK's apartment was not at all like that.

Along with that feeling I was also kind of sad. Didn't know exactly why. Maybe because of suddenly receiving something: this place in which I'd be allowed to live, without paying anything for it.

"It's a tax write-off for me," OK had said when he gave me the key.

I knew of course that I'd have to do something in return, but I chose not to worry about it just then.

For the first time in my life I'd be living not in a housing project, not in Uncle Lou's tour bus, not in a freezing cold trailer, not sharing a smelly pothead flat on the *Reeperbahn*— but in a town house on the Elbchaussee. With a river view.

Approaching the door, I could see through the glassed-in entranceway how bright it was inside. And I heard music.

I didn't think anything of it, because there was always music on in OK's apartment.

[TRACK 3]
WELCOME TO THE MACHINE

1. Because OK had programmed it.

As Mira climbed the stairs, the motion detector at the front entrance flicked on the floor lamp that stood beside the couch; also the TV, tuned to MTV.

Melody knelt on the tiled floor, stuffing T-shirts into a yellow tote bag, her cell phone wedged between her shoulder and chin.

"Oh well, if you're expecting company, it won't work out. . . . What? No, don't worry about me. Obviously . . ."

She didn't notice the TV coming on. She'd gotten used to that, because the motion detector was so sensitive, it happened all the time.

She stopped packing T-shirts. She moved the phone to her hand, glanced at the clock, and shook her head. "No, that won't be necessary. Like I said, I'm nearly done. I already brought most of my stuff to Rosa's. Listen, let's talk later. . . . I have to get on with this. Yes, tomorrow. So long. You too. So long . . ."

Melody clicked off but didn't notice Mira stopping in the doorway.

Mira set her two bags on the floor, but Melody didn't hear. She still gazed at the cell phone display.

Mira knocked on the inside of the door. Only then did Melody look up, surprised.

"Hey, Mira."

"I didn't know you'd still be here."

"I'm just leaving. I thought you were coming at four."

"Take your time," Mira said.

"OK told me you were coming at four."

"He thought you'd already moved out."

"I have, actually."

Melody stood up, shoved the cell phone into her pants pocket, and went to collect some blouses from a clothes rack.

"I need to get going. I have a show."

"In Berlin?"

"In Bergedorf. How did yours go?"

Mira pulled off her black woolen cap, walked slowly into the apartment, and looked around.

"Oh well, you know. Promo tours stress you out."

"I know."

Mira crossed toward the big glassed-in terrace. Clouds raced across the leaden sky, trees moved in the wind. You could see all the way to the Harburg Mountains.

"My goodness, it's nice here."

Melody nodded. "Yeah, I liked that view."

"So when are you going to Berlin?"

Melody didn't answer.

Mira thought, *Something's not right about this whole Berlin story*. She looked at Melody and asked, "How are things?"

Melody concentrated on trying to fold the blouses, fast, but it took a while.

There was silence between her and Mira—much too long.

Mira moved to the aquarium, tapped her finger on the glass. Some of the fish were as colorful as the butterflies in Opa's glass cases. They didn't seem much livelier, either.

"Suppose they're stunned? An electric shock from the eel?"

Melody came over to her. Now, for the first time, she looked straight at Mira. There was another uncomfortable pause. Then she pointed to the top of the bureau. "See that small tank up there? That's for the little fodder fish. Always keep a good supply. The sturgeons like them. So does the eel."

"All right."

Then, "Mira, promise me something."

"What?"

"You have to take that eel out when it gets too big."

"I will."

For a moment they stood face-to-face.

"I need to go," Melody said, and turned away.

Mira grabbed hold of Melody's tote. "Wait . . ."

Melody turned halfway. "It's not like how it used to be."

She carried a jacket over her arm that hadn't fit into the bag. Now she held it out to Mira. Black with fake fur.

"You want this? It actually belongs to the apartment. It was here when I came."

She pressed it into Mira's hand.

Mira studied its black cloth patches and said nothing.

Melody gave her an earnest look. "They wrap you up in cotton wool," she said. "But with concrete on the outside. I have to go."

"Where will you stay?"

"Everything's okay with me." She freed the tote bag from Mira's grasp, slung it over her shoulder. "Ciao." And went to the door.

"So long."

The door closed.

Mira stood alone, turned back to the aquarium. She unfolded the jacket, inspected it further, and did not look up at the small video monitor that followed Melody down the stairs.

2. I waited, looking at the jacket. I'd known it would be too big. Shook my head and went to turn off the TV.

So then I heard birds twittering and wind rushing in through the open terrace door.

I stepped outside, looked at the sky. More clouds racing past, as though in fast motion.

These lyrics from Pink Floyd's "Welcome to the Machine" went around inside my head:

What did you dream?
It's all right, we told you what to dream . . .

I told myself, *Today's the last day of Mira. Tomorrow you turn into a stranger. A stranger to yourself.* For a moment I felt like

going in the bathroom and shaving my head bald. Like they did
to traitors during some war or other.

I pictured Melody down on the Elbchaussee, heading for
the bus stop.

And I wondered, *Will she just miss the express, or still catch it?*
I hoped the latter.

Because she'd already gone through enough shit.

But I didn't want to apologize.

I thought up an explanation that seemed all right: OK is
interested in me, not in her anymore. If I'd refused the offer,
he'd have dropped her all the same. Either way, she'd have had
to move out.

Besides: She'd gotten what she wanted, or anyway,
almost. And she's tricky, she's a schemer. And she flopped....

I turned back inside. Somehow, suddenly, the apartment
seemed wrongly proportioned. Too much space, too few walls,
too much window, too little furniture.

Most likely, this was the intent. To give a cool impression.
So cool it was cold.

A stupid old ghost story popped into my head. Are there
ghosts, really? As a child, in wintertime when it got dark early,
I hardly dared to go outside, and if I did I always stayed within
range of a street lamp. That's how scared I was of ghosts.

Not that I ever saw one.

Now I paced the length and breadth of the apartment,
peering into every corner. And watched myself doing
it. Acting like a crazy person. Squatting down on the floor,

squeezing myself into the space between the sofa and the wall partitioning off the kitchen.

I thought I'd feel so safe in this apartment, and here I was, frantically searching for a nook to hide in, that's how unnerved I was!

I stopped at the aquarium. The fish were dozing, motionless, as though barely alive.

I looked in at them. And a bright little blue and yellow one stared blankly back at me.

"So how are you doing?" I asked.

He sent up a stream of bubbles.

"I take it you're well?"

He swished his tail a little.

"What are you trying to tell me? Not sure I understand."

He swished his tail a little harder.

"Oh, I see what you're getting at: A housewarming party, good idea. Could be just what this place needs. . . ."

[TRACK 4]
THE STORY OF ZUCKA
AND MELODY: PART
TWO

1. Melody didn't go to Berlin. She had nowhere to stay there and couldn't afford a hotel.

That whole Berlin story was a lie, so as not to have to say, *I'm in deep shit, have no idea how I'll go on.*

She'd spent four weeks in a clinic and hadn't let anyone know. Although Rosa, Zucka, even Mira would gladly have helped her.

Help was not what she wanted. That's why she told no one about OK taking back the apartment. But as she went down the broad steps to the Elbchaussee, she scrolled through her cell phone address book, wondering whom else she could call.

The cursor first stopped at Rosa. "Mama" Rosa had a one-room flat but would have taken her in. It would have been humiliating, though. They were close, good friends, and all. Even so, Melody needed to prove that she'd outdone Rosa, gotten further here in Germany. If she went to Rosa's now, it would be to tell about her promising future in Berlin. Not to ask her, *Please, let me stay.*

Melody scrolled on. The last name she came to was Zucka.

+   +   +

"Hey, it's been ages, where've you been hiding?"

"Are you home now?" Melody asked.

"Sure."

"Would it be okay if I crashed at your place for a few days?"

"What did you say? When would this be?"

Melody stopped walking. She could never remember if the nearest bus stop on the Elbchaussee was to the right or left. Finally she headed left.

"You know, I kind of need a place to sleep. If that would be possible."

"Sure, absolutely. When do you want to come?"

"Maybe in twenty minutes?"

"In twenty minutes?"

"Is that a problem? I could also . . ."

"Nah, not a problem."

And while Melody stood waiting for a bus, Zucka rushed around like crazy straightening up, opened the windows, made the bed, which took a while (because it was the place where he let dirty underwear pile up till there was enough to stuff into the laundry bag), shoved certain high-gloss magazines into a drawer, and noticed, as he emptied the ashtray, that the garbage can was full to the brim, couldn't hold another thing, and that it stank. He tried to take the bag out, but it was so overloaded, the bottom ripped open.

And then he heard the ringing.

He squeezed the garbage can shut, threw the kitchen window open, squirted a little deodorizer, and went to the door.

There she stood.

With a yellow tote bag over her shoulder and an embarrassed smile on her face.

2. "Of course you can stay here," Zucka said. He'd spent two years trying to get close to this woman. At times he'd had a girlfriend on the side, but he'd never really given up. Doing jobs for Papa's label, he got to see her often. He'd driven her to gigs, and when she was on tour he sent her CDs he'd burned himself with songs and upbeat sayings on them.

Then, when she'd suddenly disappeared, he'd managed to find out what clinic she was in and had gone there to see her.

And now here she was, sitting in his kitchen, studying the coffee rings on the tabletop while he made tea.

He was a little high. She was tired.

"I have a gig in Bergedorf in the morning," she said. "I'd like to get to sleep early."

"No problem," he said. "The bed's all made. I'll sleep on the sofa."

"You don't have to. Your bed's big enough for two. After all, we're grown-ups, aren't we?"

He didn't contradict her.

Zucka had a water bed, two meters long and wide.

And he had no objections to going to bed early.

For politeness' sake, he put it off for twenty minutes. In that time he washed the dishes, which was long overdue. Finally he came to her.

Melody lay on her side, face to the wall. She had on her jeans and a T-shirt. Asleep, or pretending to be.

Zucka stripped down to his boxer shorts, then lay down on his back, not too close to her, but also not too far away. He could feel her breathing, could feel her warmth.

For two whole years he'd tried to keep his love for this slender, fragile-looking girl in check. Now it flooded him, full force.

He turned toward her, slid a little closer and whispered, "Melody . . ."

She didn't answer.

He laid his hand on her arm. He felt her skin, soft and smooth. Her arm was so thin, almost like a child's. He had the feeling that somehow she was relaxing, moving backward toward him. Just a fraction of an inch, maybe.

So he embraced her from behind.

Now he knew she wasn't sleeping. They lay like spoons.

"Zucka?" She sighed.

He whispered, "I love you."

As she didn't move, he carefully began caressing her. She didn't turn, but she didn't edge away.

He couldn't have said whether he wanted more. Or whether he wanted more from life than just to keep on lying there like that forever.

He said nothing, thought nothing. He only felt her warm, soft body under the T-shirt, and he stroked the smooth skin of her upper arm.

She turned to him.

He could scarcely breathe. He held her quite tightly, but she pushed him away a bit, so that she could stroke his chest. She moved her hand down toward his belly. Then she reached her fingers inside his shorts.

Zucka could smell her smooth, soft skin. It smelled a little of lemon, and a little of sweat. He saw her large, dark brown eyes, and then saw nothing anymore.

And felt her hand on him.

He tried to say something, but all he managed was "Ahh . . ."

He could feel his blood. He stopped stroking her, dug his hands into her arms, moaned, and thought, *Never stop, just never stop.*

He opened his eyes again, stared at her, at her breasts quivering under the T-shirt.

He felt the rhythm of her hand, her body vibrating, and knew that he couldn't hold off any longer.

Or for just one more instant, one intake of breath.

He came in her hand.

Warm, rushing like a waterfall, and so beautiful, as if his soul departed from his body, flying to the angels.

He breathed, breathed . . .

For one instant the wonderful feeling lingered. Then he saw her again. She was looking at him.

He wanted to say something, but she beat him to it. She said, "There. Are you satisfied?"

He looked at her, frozen, motionless.

"Can I go to sleep now?" she asked.

She turned away. Lay on her back, looked up at the ceiling. Zucka, too, turned onto his back, rigid, clenching his teeth. Guilty of orgasm. The words *I've ruined everything* pounded like a hammer in his head.

She sighed, got up, went into the bathroom. He could hear her washing her hands. He lay there, a record playing inside his brain, repeating the same sentences: *You asshole, aching for this woman all this time, and now you've wrecked it. Coming in her hand . . . was that supposed to get her all excited? You'll never see her or lie next to her again. . . .*

He wanted to flee. He stood, longing to wipe himself. She came out of the bathroom; their glances didn't meet. He said, "I'm leaving."

"Hmm, okay," was all she said.

He'd had a slender hope for something like "Stay, it's not such a big deal. . . ."

Zucka walked out of his apartment, through the lobby, to the street, and then through Altona, past the railroad sidings through industrial zones, then through parks, to the end of the city.

He stared at the rows of neat houses in which solid citizens lay sleeping, stared at the gray pavement, at the dim streetlights.

And he thought, *It's my cock's fault! How can I ever look her in the face again?*

On a graffiti-covered park bench he saw a smashed beer bottle. He considered using its jagged edge to cut his prick off. Then he'd be free. Never horny again, no more fucking around. Finally rid of the everlasting urge.

Oh well, he thought.

He shook his head and walked on. He told himself, *It's not like I raped her, she was cool with it, and so should I be too.* Then he saw her nipples again, how they quivered under the T-shirt, and he wanted to kiss them.

Zucka made himself stop this fantasy; what good would it do? He started running past gray-faced people heading for the early shift.

When, heart pounding, he returned to his apartment shortly before eight, he was almost relieved to see that Melody was gone.

She hadn't left a note.

3. And how was it with Melody when she'd washed her hands clean and lay back down on Zucka's bed?

She was fresh out of the clinic and totally unstable, had no apartment, no money. She didn't know what would become of her. So why was she not crying?

How did it happen that after lying awake for hours, she finally did fall asleep, and woke up only when Zucka's radio alarm clock went off at seven thirty?

And when she'd let herself out to wander alone through

the city, when she'd come to a bridge and stood looking
down at the water, why did she not think about jumping in,
but trudged on—and ended up at Rosa's door?

To understand, you have to grant that hatred can sometimes be positive, a strength that sustains one when there's
nothing else.

Hatred welled up in Melody. She let it grow and grow
until it burst like an ulcer.

This hatred saved Melody's life.

Actually, Melody hated herself, or rather the hole she had
sunk in. By not asking OK to let her stay in the apartment
a while longer. By not seeking help from anyone. All she'd
done was jabber on about moving to Berlin. But she didn't
let herself in on any of this.

During that long night at Zucka's, he was the person she
hated most—Zucka, who should have realized the one thing
she needed that evening was to be left in peace. But he
hadn't. So now she couldn't stay with him anymore. Second
and third most, she hated Rosa and Kralle, snug in their own
little places, oblivious about how terrible it is, not having
anywhere to turn.

Next after them, she hated OK, who, once he saw that
her new EP would flop, had thrown her out of the apartment, who'd kindly given her a few hundred euros, just like
that. "For moving to Berlin. I wish you much success in the
capital."

And next she hated Mira, who had the apartment. And

now had a deal with OK. Mira, whose song "took off like a rocket," as OK had said. Little Mira with the chewed-off fingernails, hair dyed blue, and blank expression.

Melody hated many people. But she sensed that she should concentrate on Mira. And also that she'd better get as many people as possible on her side.

The first she sought out was Rosa.

4. Rosa would be an ally. She, too, had a long, wakeful night behind her, as always after taking on a new project at EOK Productions. She'd paced up and down for hours and dropped off to sleep on a chair in the kitchen.

Awakened by a knock, she opened the door and was astonished: There stood Melody, looking cheerful.

She'd brought fresh rolls. And wanted to talk. That hadn't happened in a long time.

"Where've you been?" Rosa asked.

Melody answered, "Zucka's. I spent the night there," knocking Rosa for a loop.

She hadn't meant to.

Rosa had been in love with Zucka right from the beginning. And she'd always felt a little hurt that he only had eyes for her friend. She had tried shrugging it off, said she was resigned to it. But no one really is resigned to unrequited love.

Melody saw Rosa looking pained, and cautiously asked, "Have you noticed how much Zucka's changed?"

"How do you mean?"

"From being together with Mira every day."

Arranging tour dates, checking on bus schedules, doing things like that for Mira was simply part of Zucka's job in Papa's studio. As Rosa knew. After all, she worked for OK too.

And being Mira's closest friend at the time, she would have known that Mira and Zucka were no more suited to each other than a mermaid to a motorbike. Or she should have known. Anyway, she made coffee.

Melody said, "Oh well, it's no wonder. Mira's changed a lot too."

Yes, of course Mira had changed, since her single had made the charts and she rushed from one promo gig to another and did interviews daily.

It would have been surprising if she had *not* changed.

But when people say that somebody has changed, they don't mean just any old way. They mean for the worse.

Melody wanted to say it but didn't: Mira's become such a phony. She doesn't care about her old friends anymore. She thinks she's better than us.

What Melody did say was, "She took the apartment away from me."

Rosa, spreading jam on a roll, said, "I thought you were moving to Berlin."

"Who told you that?" And Melody explained that she'd never wanted to go to Berlin. That Mira started this rumor to get OK to let her have the apartment.

This was nonsense. OK threw Melody out when her

contract was up. That was how it worked, as Rosa knew.

But she had gotten so little sleep that when she thought of Zucka, and Melody spending the night with him, it made her eye twitch uncontrollably.

Of course what she did not know was how things had gone, or that Zucka now sat at his kitchen table, suffering bad conscience pangs.

What she felt was that she, Rosa, never got what she truly deserved.

And that Mira obviously got everything now.

And most likely was making a play for Zucka.

And had taken the apartment away from Melody.

A rotten thing . . .

5. A stupid thing to do. About that, I admit Melo was right.

I shouldn't have moved into the apartment. Maybe not ever.

Certainly not when I did, after OK threw one of my friends out. It wasn't clear to me at the time. But later I regretted it often enough . . . because no one could be happy in that place—least of all me.

OK offered the apartment to me. And it was Rosa who encouraged me to take it, saying that I'd love it, and what a fantastic opportunity!

I should have asked Melo.

But at the time nobody knew exactly where she was.

All right, I made a mistake. And I should have tried to find out what psych clinic she was in. But I didn't. So what was I supposed to do, hang my head in shame? I did offer to help her, before. I even got her jobs. And I told her she could share the apartment with me. But she didn't want that.

I didn't really mean it about us living there together. Because she was pretty strung out. I was just trying to be nice.

While she got more and more unpleasant.

And suddenly there was this message on my phone: She absolutely had to talk with me.

So then the idiocy began. About my song "Don't Wanna Be Famous." And how I'd stolen it from her.

Here's something I caught on to later: Melody did none of that to harm me. She also did nothing to get Rosa and then Zucka on her side. Whatever she did was the result of being empty inside. Disillusioned. Because she'd always fought so hard. For a false dream.

She'd come to the end of fooling herself.

She'd believed she was a great singer, but she was only mediocre. She had talent, yes, but it hadn't been nurtured and hadn't developed.

She'd thought she was on her way to stardom, only to be booked into discos where audiences yelled, "Take it off, take it off," before she'd even sung a note. Maybe when you're starting out, you're happy about every chance to appear. But that wears thin pretty fast.

And then OK dropped her like a hot potato.

It's terrible when a bit of success is followed by total, ice-cold oblivion. And then she'd had to watch somebody else get everything she'd hoped for. And that somebody else was me. Measly Mira M. And to top it all off, I got the apartment.

As I said, moving in was a mistake. But I meant no harm.

Yet obviously she'd been greatly harmed.

Of course she could sing better than me.

But that's not what it was about.

In pop music how technically well you sing doesn't always matter. Some of the greatest rock songs have been sung by people who couldn't sing at all.

But Melody couldn't think about that—only about me getting the success that she deserved. And then suddenly she accused me of stealing her song. Or rather, she first complained that the song was about her and that it made her look bad. Which was baloney. She declared that the line "I don't wanna be a wannabe superstar" made cruel fun of her.

And she poured that whole brew into Rosa's and Zucka's ears.

And Zucka told Rosa how Mira had changed so very much. Which was true. And that she'd actually co-written that song with Melo. And that now Mira wasn't even willing to let her old friend have her share. That whole story.

And one person spread it to another, and still another, and so on.

Even the boys from the band had to listen to it all.

First everyone worried about Mira.

About Mira, who'd changed. On account of her quick success.

Although Mira really wasn't a bad person, as Rosa thought.

But Mira could be infuriating, really touchy and arrogant, as Melody thought.

Yes, she could, Rosa agreed, and chalked it up to the stress of touring.

And even Giorgio agreed, because rehearsing was often so exasperating.

The only one who knew nothing about all this was me.

Until the night of my housewarming party . . .

[TRACK 5]
IT'S MY PARTY AND I'LL CRY IF I WANT TO

1. Here's how I imagined it: An orgy—freely, wildly supercool. Zucka rolling joints galore. Melo and Kralle, dancing like crazy, like they did in discos, trashing each other and everyone there all in fun. Rosa cooking up pots of her African stew, and me and Carlo maybe doing a few songs.

I was up for it, couldn't wait for it to start. But this song line, "It's my party and I'll cry if I want to," kept playing in my head. Like the words were trying to forewarn me...

But it's easy not to pay attention. Because you'd rather not acknowledge things you're trying not to know.

Setting a date had been a problem. It was autumn 2002. Our single went gold, sold 250,000 copies! The hype was on full blast, we were booked solid, plus we had to record new material for the album. No free evening in sight for weeks!

I'd invited only Rosa, Melo, Zucka, Kralle, and the boys from the band. Because I had crowds of people around me all day, every day, and I just wanted the genuine friends I really cared about to be there and celebrate....

We needed our album, pronto. "The avalanche is rolling," OK said. "We've got to have new material *now!*" So I spent the whole day before my party was finally going to happen in the studio, me and the band.

I left a little earlier, to get the apartment cleaned up. I'd ordered a few cases of beer and some sushi.

I kicked my gym shoes under the bureau and went over to the aquarium.

"Tonight's the night!" I told the fish. They had a right to know. It was one of them, the bright little blue and yellow one sending up bubbles and swishing his tail, who'd given me the idea.

I took a bath and lay in the Jacuzzi for fifteen minutes. Then, for a joke, I put on a black evening gown. The moment I was dressed, the doorbell rang. It was the catering service.

Setting things out took five minutes.

I was pretty hungry, so I took a little sushi.

Hm. Maybe the tuna was just a bit off. Anyway, I started feeling not so good. I went out on the terrace and smoked a joint.

I came back inside, looked at the clock. Almost eight already. But I'd figured everybody would be late.

Except Kralle. Kralle was always punctual. And sure enough, when the bell rang a few minutes later, I saw her on the little monitor next to the door.

She wore her cool pinstripe suit and an eye-catching head scarf, had flowers under her arm, and grinned into the camera.

"What's wrong with you?" she asked.

"How do you mean?"

"You don't look so well."

"Thanks."

"I mean, you look exhausted."

I nodded. "I am. Besides, I think I ate something not right." I really was exhausted. "It's all just going too fast," I said.

Kralle stood looking at the sushi. I came over to her.

"You mean this stuff's no good?"

She sniffed the seaweed rolls.

"Smells normal. Delivered today?"

"A few minutes ago."

"Then it should be fine."

She took a roll, dunked it in soy sauce, put sliced ginger on, and popped the whole thing in her mouth.

"Mmm . . . Delicious."

"Maybe I just haven't eaten enough," I said, and took some tuna.

We stood there and munched.

"When are the others coming?"

"I'm wondering myself."

The phone rang.

"That'll be Zucka, saying he'll be late," Kralle said.

I answered. It was Giorgio. He called from the studio. They were still mixing a track and it wasn't getting done. "It could take a while," he said.

"First-class sushi awaits you here," I said.

"We ordered pizza."

"Oh, really?"

One hour later there we sat, just Kralle and me. And an hour after that, too. It got to be almost ten o'clock. We sat on the terrace and smoked.

I started feeling really sick. My stomach shrank into a small, painful clump. Because of how shitty this evening was turning out to be.

"Do they know this is supposed to be a celebration?" Kralle asked.

"A housewarming."

"Do you want to call them?"

I went to the phone, called Rosa.

No answer.

I tried Melody's cell. "This call cannot go through. Please try again later. This call . . ."

I called Rosa again. Five rings and I was cut off.

I stood in this huge space, at this huge table, with this little phone in my hand. Something was wrong. I knew that Rosa had hung up on me. How come? I got out my notebook, looked for Zucka's cell number, tried calling it.

After a few rings I heard his voice.

"Hey, Zucka, where are you?"

"Who's this?"

"Who d'you think?"

Silence.

"Aren't you coming?"

"To be honest . . . no."

"Hey, Zucka?!"

He hemmed and hawed.

I heard Rosa's voice: "Give it here."

It's hard on friendships when suddenly your career takes off. A day or two before the party I thought about this seriously and made a mental list of my real friends. I'd put Rosa first. Though I hadn't checked in much with her lately.

And now she was saying, "Mira, it won't happen."

"What won't happen?"

Silence.

"Rosa, what's going on?"

"As I said. Nothing's happening tonight. We're not coming."

"We, meaning who all? Where are you, anyway?"

More silence.

"How come?"

"You know perfectly well."

Now *I* hemmed and hawed. "Aw . . . Rosa . . ."

"Okay, so long," she said.

"Rosa?"

"So long." ·

End of conversation.

I went back to the terrace.

"You're even paler," Kralle told me.

I said, "Seems we get to eat all the sushi."

Kralle gave me a cigarette and a light.

We stood side by side looking at the trees, the river, the cranes, the containers.

"I kind of thought this might happen," Kralle said. "Well, maybe something not quite so extreme. But—"

"But what is it? What is going on?"

Kralle lit a cigarette from the one she'd just smoked. I took another one too, even though I felt really nauseous by then.

Kralle asked. "Are you sure you're okay?"

"What's going on with them, Kralle?"

"Oh well..."

"Oh well, *what*?"

"They're pissed off. About you moving in here after Melody
got thrown out. About you stealing songs from her. That's
what she's saying!"

"????"

"I heard it from Rosa. Melody's staying at her place now."

"Melody's staying with Rosa? What happened to Berlin?"

"She was never really going."

"She can have this place again, for all I care. I'll move back in
with you."

"That would be nice."

We stood quietly.

Somehow I wasn't ready to believe that nobody was
coming to my party.

Somehow I stupidly figured that the door would open any
moment now and everybody would come bursting in.

"So let's celebrate," Kralle said.

"There's lots to drink," I said. I threw away my cigarette.
"Come on."

MTV was on. Kralle clicked around on the remote,
switched to another channel playing something classical, in
three-quarter time. We left it on.

I mixed soy sauce with sharp green wasabi and shoved a
few bits of raw fish into myself.

Then we waltzed a few steps for fun.

Suddenly Kralle bent her knee, made me a curtsy, and said,
"Will you grant me this dance, my lady?"

She pulled me close and took the lead. I actually didn't
know how to waltz, but being in her arms like that felt good. I
relaxed, as I hadn't in a long time.

We waltzed through the gigantic space, looked at each
other, and laughed.

I reached for a beer and opened it without slowing down.
We drank it together, not stopping. I grabbed the remote,
turned up the volume, and we kept on spinning.

So what, that those idiots weren't coming, and the
boys from the band weren't done with the track? I was
happy. Although something wasn't right with my stomach. I
had a sharp, acrid taste in my mouth.

Again I thought about Rosa, the boys, that they might, no,
would still come—it wasn't even midnight yet. And I thought
about fish poisoning, because a great-uncle of mine in Yugoland
had fish poisoning one time and was in the hospital for
months and months. Maybe the sushi really was bad.

To not think about that, I pulled Kralle to me very tightly,
and we spun a little faster, and I saw things flying past me, the
trees beyond the terrace and the Elbe and the harbor cranes,
and the aquarium. And then I saw Kralle, with her black hair,
pointy nose, and the ring through the corner of her mouth.

My legs suddenly felt like pudding, and I knew I'd better sit
down. Instead I leaned on Kralle, who kept turning, and I just
turned along. . . .

And then it grew black before my eyes.

I dived off, like into a warm, soft sea.

A sea in which there were no noises, no feelings, no hunger, no sadness.

I was gone. No idea for how long.

When I surfaced I lay in Kralle's lap.

She sat cross-legged on the floor. I lay half on my side, legs pulled up, my arms around her, my face to her belly.

She was stroking my back.

It felt good—probably some sort of yoga massage. Kralle was into things like that.

I raised my head and looked into her big eyes. They shone like floodlights.

"What happened?" I asked.

"Shh." Kralle stroked my forehead.

I wondered whether to throw up. No, not necessary.

"Have I been lying here long?"

She ruffled my hair. And shone her great floodlight eyes on me.

"Those shitty fish," I said.

"You just ate too much sushi," she said.

"Not those fish. I mean the ones in the aquarium."

"What about them?"

"One of them gave me this shitty idea."

"You mean for a housewarming party?" Kralle smiled. "It's been pretty nice so far."

"True."

I sat up and looked around.

Made sure I was still here.

And suddenly I felt proud. I thought: Those idiots didn't come, just so I'd feel bad. That was what they wanted. Like, they're so important to me. But they aren't. I don't feel bad. I'm fine. Kralle's here. And if she weren't, I'd have eaten up all the sushi myself, or I'd have called someone else. My organizer was full of cool calling cards from people who'd said they'd gladly have drinks with me anytime.

I lay back down, in Kralle's lap.

"Cool that you came," I said.

"Wouldn't have missed it," she said.

2. I was not planning to start anything with Kralle. Totally never planned to start something with a woman. We just simply danced together all evening.

Later, too. When the boys from the band did finally show up and attacked the sushi, then the beer, Kralle and I danced on.

Giorgio, Hannes, and Carlo lay sprawled on the sofa getting drunk and watching us.

Oddly, their watching is what freed me. If we'd been alone, just Kralle and me, I wouldn't have let myself . . . But with them there, and Giorgio turning off the TV, playing slow-dance numbers on the stereo, and then Carlo and Hannes dancing too . . .

We changed partners a few times, but mostly I stayed with Kralle, and anyway by then the boys were clutching on to their beers tighter than onto their partners.

And then Giorgio actually played "Love Me Tender," sung

by a black vocal group so gorgeously, it made you cry, it
made you *have* to dance hip to hip, cheek to cheek, hand on
ass—and so that's what we did, Kralle and I.

Love me sweet
Never let me go

And Kralle's ass … It felt like … real … All right, I'll say it. I
got hot. It turned me on. Although I'm basically straight. But
Kralle had such soft skin, her body was so supple, and her
breasts touching mine …

I was hot for her and wanted to kiss her. But how do you
do that? I couldn't possibly start it. I'd know how if I were
slow-dancing with a guy, even if I wasn't into him that much:
I'd slowly raise my face till my mouth was near his, my lips
accidentally touching his chin.

That makes the first kiss happen.

And then the dam is broken.

But how do you do that with a woman?

I closed my eyes and fantasized wriggling my tongue into
that sweet mouth with its piercing ring. But I couldn't possibly
do that.

Finally I just stopped thinking.

And just like that, I raised my head till my lips accidentally
touched her face. Till our lips were so close to each other
that I felt her breath.

As I said, if it had been just us, I would have pulled back
right then, or maybe before. But the three boys lolling on the

sofa lit another joint, sent clouds of smoke billowing through the room, and got me high.

The whole thing felt more like a game than real. Somehow their watching us and cracking jokes made what we were doing—breathing together, mouth on mouth—feel so innocent that any first-aid instructor would have approved.

My tongue explored the soft inside of her mouth.

And hers, mine. And it was fantastic.

At some point the boys wanted to leave, and we agreed not to show up at the studio earlier than noon the next day. They laughed and told me, "Go to bed, behave yourself, be good."

Then it was just Kralle and me. At four in the morning, on the white sofa, in a tight embrace.

"I feel like I'm fourteen years old," I said. "We're fooling around and I still have my sweater on."

"That can change," she said.

Somehow I knew this had no future, and presumably not even a present. But that made no difference to me.

And while Kralle carefully took off my sweater, I tore open her pants buttons and pulled her down.

You have made my life complete
And I love you so.

3. Next morning the birds were twittering like an orchestra tuning up. The terrace door was open, and a cold wind blew in. I woke up trembling because Kralle had double-wrapped our

blanket around herself in her sleep. I actually had not thought
women did things like that.

But yes, and there are also women who snore.

I turned on my side and looked at her. Kralle has a really
pretty face, slightly slanted Asian eyes, a small, pointy nose, and
a bit of a pout. She stayed asleep, but turned to me, put her
arm over me, and gave a little grunt.

I took up my cell phone. It was ten in the morning, and
I didn't feel like sleeping anymore. I moved Kralle's arm
away—carefully, so she wouldn't wake up. I didn't want her
sweaty arm on me. I wanted her to stay asleep so I wouldn't
have to talk to her.

I sat at the big table, drank a few glasses of water, ate a
little of the white rice from the sushi, occasionally glanced at
Kralle—and that certain shitty feeling came over me.

Like always after spending the night with somebody.

Of course I was aware that every love ends with injury and
pain. But I kept on trying, starting out fresh every time. Except
somehow I couldn't get it together anymore.

Something rebelled in me.

That's putting it mildly. The thought of this person ever
touching me like that again made me physically ill. The first
night I was in bed with someone, everything was hunky-
dory. Then in the morning it was like when you're hung over.
But not from too much to drink.

Looking at Kralle, I knew one thing: I was *not* in love with
her. Just like with the underage rock guitarist I'd spent a night
with in a hotel bed. *Not* in love. I did not find him handsome.

He stank. It wasn't like it's supposed to be.

Dancing with Kralle the night before, I could have eaten her up. I was so, so hot for her. And everything that followed was beautiful.

I remember how it was when Jackson left. I was sick from loving him. I missed him so much! When Kralle and I got back from the Berlin airport, I sat out on our tiny balcony above the *Reeperbahn*. Back then I wouldn't have played Russian roulette. But I felt like I'd dissolved and was drifting farther and farther into the air like a wisp of smoke from my cigarette, or some light gas or cloud of steam. And it was not just a feeling, but like it was really happening: My body departing. And me looking on.

There's an expression—love withdrawal—and that's what every parting is. Someone pulls his love away, reclaims it for himself. And you have love-withdrawal symptoms. You throw yourself around like you're kicking an addiction cold turkey. All your thoughts go berserk and boil down to one huge craving for the drug of love.

The love that was there and now is gone. You go through every kind of shit to get it back. Like a junkie on the street, using a dirty needle, giving herself AIDS, just so she can get her fix.

People aren't interchangeable. You can't replace one person with another. But I tried to do just that. I was always in love. The boys from the band joked about it, they called me a love puppet. Giorgio once said, "Mira, you fall in love faster than anyone I know."

Yes, I fell in love fast. But by the next morning I couldn't bear it. Couldn't stay lying next to him, or in this instance, her. I split. Whoever it was didn't hear from me again.

All this waltzed around in my head while I sat at the big table in the apartment watching Kralle sleep.

I lit a cigarette, and right away felt sick again. But I finished smoking it, inhaling deeply.

When I put it out, squashing the filter into the ashtray, I saw my chewed-off fingernails and my fingertips yellowed with nicotine. My hands trembled slightly.

Right then I knew what a shrink would say was wrong with me: You're underdeveloped. Emotionally retarded. A little child. Not equipped to really feel. To have a relationship.

You cannot solve these problems with your brain—your thoughts spinning around in circles, faster, faster.

Till you're so dizzy you don't know anything anymore.

And start thinking all over again.

That is how it was with me.

I leaned back.

At that moment the phone rang.

I saw Kralle moving. I answered, quick, so she wouldn't wake up. It was Giorgio.

"Did you sleep well?"

"What's up?"

"Are you sitting down?"

"Yes. What?"

"We're invited to the MTV Awards."

I leaned farther back, looked around the apartment.

"The awards?"

"Yes, along with Robbie Williams and Madonna. Ten million people watch those."

"No, more," I heard Carlo say in the background.

"It airs worldwide."

In the background I could hear Giorgio, Hannes, Carlo, OK, and a couple of sound engineers all talking excitedly.

I brought the receiver quite close to my mouth.

"You know what, Giorgio?"

"No. What?"

"Sometimes I'm scared. The album. Everything. Scared that we won't make it."

[TRACK 6]
TRY LOVE

1. The essential thing is having a path in life. A route, an inner compass.

For me, what's essential? What makes me who I am?

As a little child, I kept looking at the floor, as though I needed to find something there. My parents took me to the doctor, because they thought something was wrong with my spine. But my spine was okay. It's just how I was: downhearted, feeling that I'd lost something.

Always looking down and looking back.

Not much later, before I started school, this other feeling took hold of me: I'm not all right. Mira is not like she's supposed to be. Something's wrong.

Even then I had this wish to dissolve, to be extinguished. I imagined myself dead, and everyone sorry—my parents, sorriest of all, standing next to my small coffin, crying. And as I imagined this, I gave a bitter laugh and thought, *Oh yes, now you're crying, but it's too late. She's gone, and it's your fault.*

My parents, they were good, they wanted to take care of me; but they were *too* good, and didn't *only* love me. They also loved humanity, and their country, and cared about a thousand other things—politics most of all. Before the trouble between Croats and Serbs began.

When there still was socialism, my parents were actively

involved in political matters. Always on the go, addressing
other people's needs. When they came home, they were
very nice to each other and to me. But something about it all
seemed false to me. This may be my earliest, oldest memory: I
felt like our whole situation somehow was a lie.

It's strange how, when you're a child, and don't yet know
what people are like, you can already sense if a person is
honest, if something about her or him feels right. And you can
instantly tell by the look on people's faces if they really mean
what they're saying.

Nothing felt worse than this falseness around me. It started
when my father first went to jail. That was still before the war.
My mother had her first nervous breakdown. Everybody smiled
at me and acted like nothing had happened. But something *had*
happened, and my life had changed forever. There was no room
for me at home. My mother even said so: She couldn't take
care of me anymore, and she wouldn't, she was just not able to.
She was too self-absorbed, too deeply in despair. Having to be
responsible for me would bring her to total collapse.

That was after the war broke out. My father lost his job and
was put in jail again. This time they didn't release him soon. And
my mother couldn't smile anymore and was taken to a clinic.

I got sent to Oma's. But I didn't feel all right there, either.

To my grandma I was the child of the man who had
destroyed her daughter's life.

Then I realized that I alone, and no one else, was responsible
for me. Of course I didn't tell this to myself in those words,

because that isn't how you think about such things at that age. But I arranged my life accordingly: I played alone, had conversations with myself, built a make-believe world of my own. And when I didn't feel like playing anymore, I hunkered down into a nameless melancholy—a not unpleasant kind of pain, if such a thing can be.

The only solution to my problems I could imagine was dying. I remember coming back from shopping with Oma one time, I saw people going by, carrying the coffin of a young man who'd died in the war. His parents and relatives followed, all crying. Oma, who really didn't take much pleasure in living herself, said, "If only they'd carry me away too." I was seven years old. And inwardly I wished it too, with my whole heart, as though I'd suffered the greatest sorrow.

And so one's personality develops.

Later, when I was very anxious, the therapist defined my condition: Borderline. Always on the edge. Underlying causes: depression—also grandiosity. On the one hand I was sad, withdrawn, felt inferior to everyone; but at the same time I imagined that I was someone quite special, with extraordinary abilities. As a child I believed I had magic powers. Like a witch or a prophetess. I believed that I could make that yellow lemon butterfly from Opa's collection come back to life, take wing, and fly away.

In my fantasies I was a heroine, but my real life—with my parents, with Oma, then in Germany with Uncle Lou—looked very different. Back in Croatia, I was the Serb; in Germany, the Yugoslav. But that wasn't what was so bad. The problem was me.

I wanted to have friendships, was often on the verge of pouring my heart out to someone. But I never did. Because I didn't trust other kids and had no one to depend on.

I'd enter a schoolroom and no one even said hello. Kids got together in the afternoons, everybody glad to see everybody else, except me. Already then, Mira was really almost not there.

You get used to it, but it still hurts. Until you realize, well, that's how you are: invisible. And you may think it's better that way, because that way you don't get made fun of.

That's the worst thing: getting laughed at. Worse than getting cursed or beaten up. And it started happening, more and more. No matter what I did, and even when I just sat in a corner of the school yard by myself...

In class, if I answered a question, everybody burst out laughing. Even the teacher. And later they'd discuss what was so funny about what I'd said.

Then when I was alone, during recess or at home, I made fun of myself, because obviously I was ridiculous.

Where did this come from? Was it my looks? Okay, I was pretty small, but was that so comical? Was it that I spoke with an accent? I trained myself to lose it pretty fast.

That didn't change anything.

The reality: Somehow I was lame inside and could not deal with other people. That was why I held back. Inhibition. It wasn't just my chewed-off fingernails, or the stupid way I wore my hair that people found so comical. I was ridiculous. Maybe you wouldn't believe it if you'd met me later on. But that is how it was.

Or something like that.

Then Uncle Lou rescued me a second time: He put a guitar
in my hands.

And I became a punk rocker.

2. It was my eleventh birthday. As usual, he hadn't gotten me a
present and felt bad about it. So he picked up an electric guitar
and said, "Here, for you."

Of course the guitars Uncle Lou kept around were pretty
fantastic—it was a shame to give one to a girl who'd never
held anything like it in her hands: a Fender Stratocaster,
handcrafted (sigh!). Sunburst, from yellow to red, and a dark
neck with mother-of-pearl inlays.

This he handed to me. And then of course he had to give
me lessons. Uncle Lou was a brilliant teacher. Whatever knack
I had for playing guitar, I owe to him.

The time with him was like a maelstrom. When he was
between gigs, he'd bellow at me over the least little thing. Like,
one day I came home from school so hungry I had stomach
cramps, and I asked him if he could give me money to go buy
something to eat. Because there was no food in the house for
a change.

And he had a screaming fit, about how much money I cost
him, how my parents didn't give him a penny for my keep. And
if I weren't the daughter of his neurotic sister... And so on.

That was the first time I wanted to clear out, never speak
to him or even look at him again, just get away—it didn't
matter where to.

Lots of times he'd lie on the sofa dead drunk. But other

times he'd spend hours helping me with homework, cooking
things for me. And teaching me how to play really mean
electric guitar. Some evenings, when his girlfriend came home
from work, we'd be like a regular family. She wanted me to
call her Aunt, let me sit on her lap when we watched horror
videos (and when it got too gruesome, she covered my eyes).

Sometimes it happened that I'd get up in the morning and
the two of them were lying on the floor in the foyer in an
alcoholic stupor after half demolishing the whole place. Uncle
Lou did all kinds of drugs, especially on tour.

Touring was the coolest. He always took me along during
summer vacation, and other times too, when he had his
own band again. In Croatia he was a star, the rocker Udo
Lindenberg of the Balkans. Here in Germany nobody knew
his band, but down there he had fan clubs. In Hamburg he
did studio musicians' jobs, playing whatever promotion songs
happened along, but down there he rocked the biggest
concert halls. And I went along. The guys in his band had
tattoos, wore leather, and were very nice. I slept in a sleeping
bag behind the stage, or in the tour bus, and played poker
every night with the roadies. They let me take sips of their
whiskey and the occasional toke.

The first time I got high, I laughed so much, I couldn't stop,
even after the concert, in the hotel, and Uncle Lou cursed me
out for being too young.

I stayed with him till just before my thirteenth birthday.

I hadn't planned to split, there was no good reason to,

except the summer—and with it, touring—was over. I'd felt good being with other punk rockers, not like an outcast anymore, because we were all outcasts together. And if you obey the rules—the punk rock scene has some, all music scenes do—then you're accepted, you belong.

If you're a punk rocker and take off on your own, you'd better not be sixteen yet, because then it's forbidden, you're breaking the law. But if you're almost thirteen it is the coolest thing to do. And to be cool was what I wanted. On the road I'd heard a lot about what's cool.

Uncle Lou was in one of his rages, yelling and screaming at me, because I'd picked the wrong moment to stand in the wrong place: blocking his light while he noodled around on his guitar. Also—this is probably what set him off—he'd misplaced a guitar string, couldn't find it anywhere.

He yelled for an hour—or who knows how long? Finally his girlfriend pulled him off me, because they were supposed to go out and she'd been waiting all that time.

So then they left and I stayed behind, alone. I took Lou's guitar and unstrung it. Outside it was getting dark. Tomorrow I'd have to go back to school, where everyone would give me a hard time. I looked out the window for a while. Then I collected my sleeping bag and my savings account book, took a hundred mark from the household money, and in the stillness said, *So long.*

Everything else I left behind—my guitar, and even the brooch from my mother. I caught the bus to the *Autobahn*, and I'll never forget how I felt when I got there. What a moment! It was such a high. . . . I stood by the entrance ramp, next to a cement bridge, the sun setting bloodred, and I screamed with joy.

The first car that stopped I got into—wherever it was headed, fine with me. Somehow I made it to Dortmund that night, ran through the street, ended up at a punk concert. Don't know how I managed to luck out like that.

I crashed in one of those punk houses. Next morning, while everyone was still asleep, I raided the refrigerator, then took off, caught a bus to the *Autobahn* again.

Being on the road . . . it was one long dream. Sometimes I'd wake up, look around—aha, so here's where I am—and sink back into the dream again.

The first evening, standing at the entrance ramp, that was the peak moment. And another, when I met my sweet fifteen-year-old punk rocker in Essen. Low points came later, plenty of them. I'd started doing speed and snorting coke—that was horrible, gives you instant anxiety attacks. I had scabies, I was hungry, went to bed with nasty guys.

But going back to Uncle Lou was totally out of the question.

At some point I woke up on the outskirts of Hamburg, in Altenwerder, where the container harbor was, and lucked into the *Bauwagenplatz*, with the long-haired hippie jerk-offs. There I found a new home.

Kralle took care of me.

And it slowly dawned on me that someone to care was what I needed.

+   +   +

3. On the evening after the catastrophic housewarming party,
after the first night with Kralle, I walked through the city
alone . . . stopped on every bridge and stared down at the Elbe,
the dirty gray water flowing lazily along. . . .

Next to Venice, Hamburg has the most bridges of any city
in Europe.

On every bridge, when I looked down, I thought, *Why don't
you jump? Better than staying so miserable and always alone . . .
Why not tie a clump of cement to your foot and throw yourself in?*

Very simple: because that clump of cement wouldn't stay on.

And if you jumped in anyway, you wouldn't sink. Or if you
did, and hit bottom, got all smashed up, and had the bad luck
to live on, in a wheelchair for another fifty years . . . I didn't
have the heart for that.

And that was why, the fourth time my cell phone rang, I
finally picked up. And saw her name on the display . . .

Kralle.

The first time it rang I just let it. As always after the night
with someone.

Also the next two times it rang.

But then I answered.

Had to. Gave it another try, at least.

Try love

"Hello, Kralle?!"

[TRACK 7]
STARDUST

1. My first hotel room, on Mira M. and the Spiders' very first promo tour, was the size of a phone booth. But I was thrilled. It had cable TV. And for breakfast there was a buffet.

From then on, night after night, hotel after hotel. Soon no more crummy ones, but Marriotts or InterContinentals. You collapse onto the synthetic bedspread with its chemical smell, and if you forget to turn the air-conditioning off, you wake up next morning with a bad cold and no voice. And sweet little twelve-year-old girls who'd traveled hundreds of kilometers to the concert chasing after me, trying to catch me on the phone. Which didn't happen, because I'd learned to unplug mine.

It all got to be routine. Less fun, more and more stress. Signing autographs is like addressing envelopes in an office. Except the addresses change, but your name is the same over and over again.

If there was a break and you got home for a few days, there was laundry to do, and catching up on sleep. Then you'd have to pack again. And when you needed to buy stuff, people in the supermarket would push and shove to get near you. Some would stare you right in the face, then quickly look away. Others would peer into your cart to check out what you were buying.

What really got to me was all those young girls wanting to

look like me, imitating how I dressed, down to the last detail!
I'd stand in the check-out line and see a girl come in, same
color hair, same outfit, even the same shoes—it struck me as
so pathetic.

When I felt totally unhinged, I'd go to some Asian store and
load up on those soups from Hong Kong and Thailand with
the sharp, spicy noodles that we used to eat raw, right out of
the bag.

It took me back to when I hung out with Rosa and Kralle
every day or played guitar for hours.

My life was a roller coaster, or like a Formula One race at
uncontrollable speed, chasing other cars around and around in
circles, not reaching any goal.

Or else the chasing *was* the goal.

And by the way, it didn't make me rich. I earned just enough
to live on.

But everybody thinks, well, now you're swimming in money,
and people regularly hit on you for handouts. Melody the
worst, of course. She bombarded me with phone calls. Like a
stalker.

And now she claimed there was a cassette proving that I'd
stolen "Don't Wanna Be Famous" from her. A small cassette,
she said, the kind that was used in minirecorders. She wanted
to come to the apartment and look for it. So we could listen
to it together.

There actually was that kind of recorder, a relic from the

predigital age, in OK's apartment. And cassettes for it in
various places. I played some. Nothing on them, just static.
Some were still in their wrapping.

I wanted to go out and be normal again, go to clubs like
a regular person. I knew that some friend of Zucka's was
appearing at the Basement. I figured they'd all be there—
Melody, Rosa, Zucka. I missed them, at least Rosa and Zucka.
So I went.

He was the first one I saw. Right in front of me. I said, "Hey,
Zucka!"

He gave me a stare, turned around, walked away.

Not a word, not even hello.

Then I also spotted Rosa and Melody.

My bosom friends. Zucka was talking to them, pointing in
my direction. They grabbed their jackets and pocketbooks
and left.

I felt like miserable little Mira all alone during recess again.

When you become famous, people point fingers at you about
stuff you have nothing to do with. Okay, I'd crossed Melody
off the list of people I thought were my friends. But why
were Rosa, and Zucka, too, acting like I'd committed some
unpardonable crime?

Rosa obviously was miffed that now we only saw each
other in OK's office, when she was working on something of
mine. And she always said, "Let's get together soon." And we
didn't. But that was because I really had so little time.

Okay, my fault for not calling. But that used to not bother her, before.

One time I did call her to make up, but I said things I shouldn't have. Then she started in about how I'd changed so much, told me what Melody and Zucka and also other people were saying and thinking about me. It pissed me off, and I said, "Do you think your opinions are that interesting?"

When Rosa didn't answer right away, I added, "D'you think *you* are that interesting?" She hung up.

I stood in my giant apartment, at the huge table, and said under my breath, "I don't need any of you."

I'm alone, I always was. So what? I'm alone, and I'm strong, I've done what I wanted to do.

That is what makes me different, I thought: Melody flopped. Rosa sorts mail in OK's office. Zucka will never make it as a rapper. But I made it, I got there, with my own songs, my own ideas. And that's why they all envy me.

I had nothing to reproach myself for. I'd done nothing shameful, like crawl up some producer's ass, or strip, or let them weigh my breasts.

I'd gotten there without any of that.

And I wasn't finished. Not by a long shot.

2. OK thought my thing with Kralle was great—a lesbian friendship and like that. "It'll be a first-class boost to sales," he said.

Right! I'd gradually caught on that he wasn't as big as he made himself out to be, and that I was already too big for his dinky label. EOK Productions meant ten or twelve people. I could probably get myself a better deal.

Anyway, Kralle. Sure, I had mixed feelings. Even so, being with her was the best time in the apartment. She was the reason I could bear all the crap. She picked me up at the airport, brought me home, listened to everything, all my problems and stories. Even when I told about meeting up with some sweet guy or other.

She also got me the X and speed I needed. Although it worried her. Not that I was a total junkie. Really not.

She still had the pad on the *Reeperbahn*. But I was fine with her eating and sleeping at my place anytime. Why not? She did so much for me. And when we went out to places that she couldn't afford, I'd pay her way.

It really was okay with me. But not with her. It bothered her. She didn't want to be "kept."

A bigger problem was my jealousy. Totally irrational. I knew that she was faithful to me. And I was to her—but only because nothing as good turned up. I'd have cheated on her instantly if Mr. Right had come along.

She sensed it, of course. Women feel those things. Besides, we didn't see each other all that much, and when we did I often was preoccupied, someplace else inside my head. When we went out, there were always crowds of people dying to talk to me. And Kralle would stand and watch. She wanted us to have time for each other, she wished I'd take a break.

"You know, OK has quite a lot of money invested in me," I said. "I can't take off just like that."

That was a lie. I didn't want to.

Then she'd say that I looked pretty much done-in sometimes. "Take a look at yourself in the mirror," I said back.

I thought I was being especially smart and honest when I threw hurtful things at her. Called her a loser, told her to think about her future, things like that. Anyway, I was probably right when I said that her scribbling wasn't going anywhere.

Kralle wanted to be a writer, but I didn't take that seriously.

I made jokes about her, ignored her, flirted with others in front of her. And then if she complained, I told her in all earnestness that *she* had a problem with jealousy, that she was incapable of accepting me as I was, and blah blah blah.

When *I* was the sicko-jealous one! And made her life a hell when she all innocently got together with a friend.

When she said this to me, I somewhere deep inside felt she was right. But I didn't admit it, I just wasn't able to.

Seeing her unsure of herself, hurt, and fearful, I started to really despise her. Suddenly she wasn't the least bit attractive anymore. And I thought, *What do I need her for?*

I felt powerful, and I said things that I didn't really mean.

"Look for someone else. I don't need you anymore." Yes, Mira said those things.

Yes, that was bad of me. But she stayed all the same. That was her fault, not mine.

Emotional co-dependency is what it's called. Me depending on her, and she on me.

That's what the good-looking therapist said.

Could be. But emotional co-dependency also feels good. No, bad, but in a way that does feel good. Like how your next fix feels if you're addicted—very good. Fantastic.

Such co-dependency between two people doesn't make for happiness and should be avoided. But the other kind of love, the healthy kind, coming from your heart and soul—that just never was my thing.

After we'd quarreled, and I'd cursed her out, we held each other close, we kissed, and both of us felt, No, I don't want to lose you, not even when it's terrible....

Those were fantastic moments.

I could have been different, but I didn't want to make the effort. I wanted to stay as I was, although I wasn't happy. But I only realize that now—when it's too late.

And why did Kralle put up with all that? All the hurts she said she could not bear?

Because she was scared. Scared she'd lose me. And why? She was scared of losing her own self.

I was scared of losing myself in her, and held her at a distance. And she was scared that she'd lose herself if she lost me. Both of us being so scared was actually what held us tied together.

Which brings me to the MTV Awards.

3. Because before I could come hurtling down, the roller coaster kept on climbing. To the pinnacle. The MTV Awards, live from Barcelona, seen worldwide on TV. It's like the Oscars are for movies. Even really successful people who've worked for years and years don't get that far.

Before, when I'd watched the show on TV, I got depressed, because I was sure that I'd never make it. That such success just wasn't meant for me, not in my lifetime.

And now—on the morning after my housewarming and the night with Kralle—the invitation came! *The* big opportunity for our international breakthrough, OK said. The White Stripes were scheduled to play, also The Darkness. Christina Aguilera hosting. Nominees were Robbie Williams, Justin Timberlake, Beyoncé. And lots of others. And me, us: Mira M. and the Spiders! Category: Best German Act, along with Xavier Naidoo and *Die Ärzte* (The Doctors).

We rehearsed for weeks, developed a whole new version of "Not in a Thousand Years," with acoustic guitar and synthetic string players. Supersentimental.

We took an early-morning flight to Barcelona, spent the whole day sightseeing, the Spiders and me, Mira M.—who a year ago was living in a crash pad on the *Reeperbahn*, and whose demo CD had landed in the trash. And now, with a TV camera team behind us, here we were, strolling down Barcelona's most elegant street, Las Ramblas, feeling like we owned it.

And . . . come evening, we played in this enormous hall before all those celebrities. This was it, the thing you're always dreaming of. Now it was real—and a huge letdown!

It didn't glow.

The dressing rooms so sterile, the dreary corridors, and

all those TV people crowding us, the interviews we had to
do, quick, quick ... it all felt dim to me, as though I was seeing
everything through a gray veil.

Maybe because the antidepressant I'd been taking wasn't
working. Or maybe because I was exhausted. So I took a little
speed, but that didn't help.

No. It was the occasion. No real audience, no real rock 'n'
roll—not so different from promo gigs, only bigger, and people
wore fancy evening clothes and drank from champagne glasses
instead of beer mugs.

I stood on that gigantic stage, and it was like I wasn't there.
No contact with what audience there was, on account of all
those camera guys horsing around in front of me, and having
to hurry, get through your two songs fast and get off. At least
there was a little dry-ice fog. But not even that was cool.

We played "Famous," which by that time I'd had up to here.
Oh, we were good, and things went smoothly, the Spiders
rocked, I played, I sang, the camera people smiled at me, there
was a classy light show, and behind me a giant video wall with
my face on it. . . . The audience applauded, cheered. . . .

And it was just nothing. A big emptiness.

To know that umpty millions are watching ...

It wasn't what I'd waited for. And then you're done, you go
offstage, Christina Aguilera's out there, already announcing the
next act, and all these people crowd around you. Journalists,
TV types, wannabe celebs, women with too much makeup on,
guys wearing striped ties and smelling of coffee and stomach
acid. So many empty faces. And all these eyes, shining with

adulation. And everybody saying the same things: "Wonderful, fantastic, *wunderbar*, great, *fantástico*, I was so moved, I almost cried, you play a cool electric guitar, so authentic, hilarious."

And when they turn around they pack up their adulation—they're stingy with it, save it for the next occasion.

Later, when we were sitting in the bar swilling champagne and tequila with the tech crew and the German hip-hoppers, things felt good to me again. The award for Best German Act went to *Die Ärzte*. Oh well. Who cared? They were off celebrating in some elegant hangout with the suit-and-tie-and-heavy-makeup people.

The underground bar we sat in was in the old city of Barcelona, Spaniards and Catalans all around us. I snuggled up to Giorgio, did some screaming, spilled beer, went to the toilet, snorted coke.

At some point Snowflake came along. He was in this group, the East Berlin Rappers, all very cool types, straight from the ghetto, like Zucka wished he could have been.

Flakey was big, broad-shouldered, like he lifted weights, played basketball. He rolled a joint, then looked at me and said, "Actually, punk's not my thing, but you were cool."

At some point we went outside and did a little coke. And I thought, *Don't get involved with this one, Mira. It'll set you back. He's one of those homies with nothing much to say besides "Yo, man," and "Where's the beer?" and "Gimme a drag."*

But he had lightning in his blue eyes. . . .

I went back in and joined the others, so as not to start something stupid right there.

+   +   +

I noticed I was trembling. Things had been so rough these last few months; I'd been pretty stoned for quite a while. And now I had champagne, tequila, joints, speed, coke, and beer all mixed together inside of me.

Plus, my antidepressant. I guess I'd miscalculated how it all would interact. Anyway, I kind of OD'd, which is why I took a few drags off another joint and had another beer, to bring me down a bit.

But it also felt pretty good.

I leaned against Giorgio some more; that was safe. The hip-hoppers beatboxed and freestyle rapped about this crazy day. We were among ourselves, and we were the greatest. Mira M. and the Spiders from Venus. Coolest German newcomers in ten years, that's what Aguilera said.

It was the kind of evening when you suddenly get an urge to jump up on the table and yell something nonsensical. And that's what I did.

"Hello, people, I have something to say!"

At first nobody paid any attention.

I drummed my heels on the tabletop. Finally people quieted down, at least those near us.

"Mira M. has a statement to make!" I shouted.

Now there really was silence, everyone in the whole place fell quiet—except for one "Yo man" from the hip-hop posse.

I felt all those eyes on me, but what was it I wanted to say?

"People, I think I need to throw up."

Everyone cheered, egged me on, "Go ahead, do it!"

I pressed my index finger to my lips, went "Ssshhh!"

When there was silence again, I said, "I hereby announce the end of my career. I'm canceling all future appearances."

They didn't believe me, thought I was joking. I myself had no idea how close it came to being true.

I babbled on: "The career of Mira M. is ended. I declare the Spiders dissolved. I'm staying here in Barcelona. . . ."

I bent down, grabbed a beer bottle, and took a swig.

That rapper, Snowflakey, the one I'd snorted coke with, leaned forward and said, "Fantastic panties you've got on."

I sat down in the middle of the tabletop and finished the beer. The Spaniards and Catalans at the other tables turned away, started yakking. They hadn't understood a word I'd said.

Giorgio leaned toward me. "Hey, what's with that shit?"

"Never say shit to me."

"Mira, you can't quit now."

"I won't. All great rock stars say they will, every year. And they go on anyway."

"Okay, I'm reassured."

"Now will you all kindly excuse me? I have to go vomit."

I went straight through the room to the toilets, though my legs were kind of wobbly, and my only thought was, *Can I hold off till I get there?*

Yes, I did.

4. I taxied back to the hotel with Giorgio. But somehow that guy Snowflakey had finagled himself into my room.

It was nice with him, I admit.

We did nothing very bad, I was too wasted. We spent the whole next day together. That was the first vacation day I'd had in a whole year.

The coolest thing was, nobody seemed to recognize me. In Germany I was a star, but in Spain our CD wasn't even out. Snowflake and me, all morning we wandered through the city just like ordinary tourists. And in the afternoon we took a taxi to a little town by the sea.

There I lay on the beach, on his muscular upper arm, watching the clouds go by. Man, it was November, and so warm, we could have swum. I jumped to my feet, rolled up my pants, ran to the water. Fishermen in light blue boats were emptying their nets. Beside one of the boats I found a little seahorse. It lay wriggling in the sand.

Ah, that little seahorse. I should have rescued it... brought it back, put it in the aquarium. But I didn't. Just like I should have taken the eel out of there, as I'd promised I would, but didn't... Oh well...

Our flight took off that evening. I'd gotten rid of Snowflake— quite elegantly, I thought.

We landed in Hamburg around midnight. OK and a small gathering met us at the airport.

Then there was another celebration in another jolly bar not so different from the one in Barcelona. Except you had to be wearing something warmer than a T-shirt. And you ran into people you knew.

More champagne, speed, joints, tequila, beer, on top of my antidepressant. All that. And I was still high from the night before.

I ended up in the toilet, puking again.

Surrounded by girls trying to get at me, I studied my face in the mirror. Now I really looked like those promo photos: black-rimmed eyes, though not from makeup. Totally pale, very thin. And I asked myself: *When will you come crashing down?*

I left the bar before the others, not saying good-bye.

I wanted to get home, walked to the taxi stand.

Then I saw her.

That tall, slender figure, that walk, the stiff way she held her neck—I knew right away, I could *feel* who it was.

Although I didn't see her clearly. It was too dark, and kind of drizzly. But she came nearer, as if through a beam of light.

At three a.m., coming toward me at the taxi stand. The last person in the world I wanted to run into.

Melody, who'd hounded me these many months, insisting I stole "Famous" from her. The very song that she herself at one time called shitty!

There she was. Long leather coat. African-style hairdo, lots of little braids. She looked enchanting, as always.

I asked myself, *How did this happen? Has she been waiting here, to catch me?*

This was the first time we'd actually stood face-to-face since I'd moved into the apartment.

Which, as I've said, I regretted. I made up my mind to be

pleasant. Although I felt like throwing up again. I managed "hello" nicely.

She said nothing.

If there was one thing Melody was good at, it was saying more by being silent than with a thousand words. She could cut you up into little snippets with her eyes.

I asked, "Did you see the show?"

"Nah. How was it?"

I was sure she'd seen it.

"Cool," I said. "A little too cool, to be honest. The award went to *Die Ärzte*."

We stood at the curb. Next to a burned-out trash can. The taxi drivers looked us over, wondering, When will they finally get in?

"How are things with you?" I asked.

All she said was, "Why don't you pick up when I call you?"

I was chilled, I was dead tired, OD'd. "What is it you want?" I asked.

"Only what is mine."

"And that is?"

"My share."

"Okay. How much do you want?"

"Only what's coming to me. The contract. And the copyright."

In other words, everything.

I was ready to give her something . . . But not everything. I'd worked long and hard on that song. I, and I alone.

"Nothing less will do?"

"Give me the contract and copyright, and I'll leave you the performer's fee."

Man, how generous!

I got into a taxi by myself.

She stood on the curb. "You're a coward, Mira. And a liar," she cried after me.

The taxi got going. I felt like calling Kralle. But I'd deleted her number the last time we quarreled, and now I couldn't remember it. I put my cell phone away.

I dozed off as we drove through the dark city. The taxi driver had his radio on, very low, and I could hear the woman dispatcher explaining some complicated address, and other voices, short sentences, snatches of conversation. I drowsed again, half woke up, in a fog, still hearing low voices.

And then in the apartment, as I lay on the big white sofa, I heard a rushing in my ears, and I thought: *You'd better shut the terrace door before you fall asleep.* But I kept lying there, staring up at the ceiling. And then I heard them. Voices. Very low, like on the taxi radio, speaking in short sentences, saying inscrutable things.

But the taxi radio wasn't on, not here in the apartment. At first I thought, *Maybe it's the TV, or else the radio.* But they weren't on. And the voices still came and didn't go away. Not when I put wax earplugs in, nor when I put my headset on.

Hello . . . are you still there?

Hello . . . are you still there?

Hello . . . are you . . .

I want to get into my corner. . . .

Orange is nice. . . . Orange is nice. . . .

Where are you? Are you still there?

We are inside your head.

I thought: *Mira, be calm, you're worn out, you didn't sleep last night, so you'd better sleep now.* But I didn't. I lay there on the sofa, in my clothes, and outside it was still dark. I felt like I was made of glass. And the voices murmured right by my ear.

I thought: *It will be dawn soon. Then they will stop.*

But they did not. . . .

[TRACK 8]
INNER VOICES

1. I feel so afraid.

That I'm going crazy.

That something is wrong with my brain.

That something is wrong with *me*.

And that this fear will never stop.

Fear of dying. Fear of living like this. Fear of going out on the street. Fear of people. Fear of being alone.

When the voices weren't there, I listened for where they were. Till they came back again.

What was that just now?

That fish will eat you up.

Do you believe in wonders? Wonders? Wonders? Wonders? Wonders?

You can trust me. You can trust me.

What did you do yesterday?

You can trust me.

What did you do yesterday?

Flopped.

What did you do yesterday?

What did you do yesterday?

I'd been having symptoms for a while: eye twitches that grew worse and worse, bouts of dizziness that sent me reeling,

made me sick as a dog. And when I was on speed, endless
monologues inside my head.

The voices. They're back. . . .

I stand in the apartment, everything here is too big, and it's
a mess. Clothes all over the place. And all those cell phones . . .
who needs a new one every other week? And stuff—fan mail,
posters from our latest tour, press clippings, and all the other
mail one gets.

I stand there, gape at the fish in the aquarium, and my heart
starts racing.

I'm afraid that I can't hack it.

Afraid I'll need a lobotomy, like those guys in *One Flew Over
the Cuckoo's Nest*, wearing a stupid grin and a thick scar across
my forehead.

Kralle said lobotomies aren't done in Germany anymore.
But somewhere I read that electroshock is coming back.

Fear raged in me like a tornado, ice-cold, not letting up,
that's all I knew.

I didn't know where it came from, or where it was headed.

Hearing voices means you lose your body, doesn't it?
Means you lose your own self, where you live. Lose the floor
beneath your feet. Lose the legs you walk with, lose your arms,
your hands . . .

"My heart is sore pained within me: and the terrors of
death are fallen upon me . . . /Oh that I had wings like a dove!/
For then would I fly away, and be at rest."

Yes, I started to read the Bible, the Psalms. There are some
good song texts in there.

+   +   +

Hearing voices is a classical symptom of schizophrenia, said
one neurologist I saw.

Kralle made me go to him. She brought me to his office.

Paranoid-hallucinatory schizophrenia is an incurable illness,
the neurologist said. There are medications that help suppress
the symptoms. But along with the symptoms, they suppress
most everything else. I knew this without him: You turn into
an apathetic, listless, swollen sad sack and sit in the corner and
drool.

"A brief psychotic disturbance." That's what he said I had.
Because the voices always went away after a few days.

And because auditory hallucinations were the only
symptoms I presented, the diagnosis could also have been
"unspecified psychotic disturbance."

"Severe stress syndrome," was what another neurologist
said.

Of course my symptoms could have had bodily causes too.

Or be drug-induced.

We went to doctors, psychiatrists, psychologists. OK had
canceled all my concerts and studio dates, saying, "You first
need to get free of all those."

I tried a homeopath, too. The initial conversation, where
you tell your whole life and every illness you ever had, was the
best thing about that. I learned things, listening to myself. He
gave me some little round pills, but they did nothing.

All I knew after consulting these medical experts was that

they don't really know much themselves. There are as many opinions as there are doctors. They found all sorts of illnesses I never felt sick from or knew I had: My heart was not quite right. Mitral valve prolapse syndrome or something. One lung was too flat, and my hearing a bit weak—most likely from the concerts.

When I was alone, the hissing and whispering in my eardrum came on again. The voices, the fear. And then nothing worked anymore. It was like you sit there, or stand, or lie, it doesn't matter which, and you're freezing cold, and sweat runs out of all your pores, and things around you look all foggy, or like they're made of cotton wool.

Finally Kralle convinced me to check into the psych clinic. That sounds dramatic. But it wasn't. The patients weren't hopeless cases. It was like a hospital for psychosomatic stuff. For me it was a break, time out. Imaginative meals, nice conversations. And I was in the park a lot, taking good long walks.

Anyway, it helped more than all those doctors. I learned to tell the symptoms apart, and how to try to deal with them. The voices mostly came when I lay down exhausted, stressed out, eyes closed, and couldn't rest.

If I remembered that they'd stop at some point, they mostly did. And this was progress.

If they refused to, I stood up, drank a glass of water, ate something, looked out the window. Then they stopped. Or I could drown them out with music.

Fear was the bigger problem, and the clinic people couldn't

help me with that, said the terrific-looking young psychologist.

They let me out, sent me home.

2. A creative pause, that's what we called the clinic time and
after; it was really forced on me, like injury pauses for soccer
players when they're so overtrained and burned out, they tear
a tendon or a muscle in some harmless situation.

Something in my brain had torn, and it slowly had to heal.

So said the very handsome psycho-uncle. I kept going to
him, and he listened to me for an hour twice a week.

The voices, he explained, result from something the brain
misinterprets. Like when you have a conversation with
yourself, just quietly, internally. And if the brain is under
total stress, it attributes these inner voices to an outside
source.

"And just as your brain has learned to make these
misinterpretations, it can unlearn them," he told me.

That did not make everything better.

The good thing was, no obligations—no performances, no
studio dates. I could stay home a few weeks.

"You have to create situations for yourself in which you feel
comfortable," the psycho-doc had said.

Sit on the terrace, practice guitar a little, write in my diary,
cook something delicious with Kralle . . .

"You have to figure out what helps you. . . ."

Cold was what helped me. A cold shower. Holding ice
cubes in my hand. Stripping down to my T-shirt, standing out
on the terrace in the middle of winter.

When I told that to the therapist, he said, "You shouldn't overdo it."

But I did. I left the terrace door wide open, turned the heat off, got undressed, and settled myself on the sofa. It was below zero outside then, and inside not much warmer. I'd sit like that for hours, buck naked. The harsh light made my skin look even bluer. I felt nothing anymore.

Kralle was shocked when she found me like that one day. Shut the terrace door, turned the heat on. Made warm tea.

I didn't feel like drinking it.

Sometimes I just bent over the aquarium and held my head underwater till I urgently needed to breathe.

I let the cold water from my hair run down over my body.

I shivered and had gooseflesh, but I also felt a little better.

One time, in the midst of such an anxiety attack, I stood before the mirror and confronted the fear, tried looking it straight in the eye.

Then I shut my eyes. I had to.

Fear rampaged inside me. It was awful, unbearable, but I stayed with it. I endured it. And at that moment I felt something new beginning. Something bright. A light, quite small and weak. But it didn't go out. No, it didn't.

On that day, I wrote this song:

Stars—tumbling over my head
Falling into my head
Falling into my heart

Stars—that's what he gave
That's what we are...

And so on.

It was a beautiful song.

Later, we recorded it too.

"You have to learn how to trust your body again," as the psychologist had said.

And Kralle...

3. Kralle was getting on my nerves. Being bossy. Interfering. Telling me I shouldn't do speed, or even pot.

OK had us start planning new tour dates for spring. And Kralle got outraged. "You're letting yourself in for that whole craziness again?"

It was strange. I'd gladly have chucked it. No more Mira M. and the Spiders. I'd spent eight months on that roller coaster. Wasn't that enough? Why did I give in to OK, and start all over again?

Studio sessions, promo gigs, TV appearances, interviews, hardly sleeping... I'd learned what that would do to me. But Kralle butting in... that made me want to lash out. I told her she was jealous of my success.

She said, "No, I'm proud of you. And I'll be so happy every time I see you on TV. I'm just scared you'll overdo it."

"You can stay where you are, namely nowhere," I said. "Me, *I* want to get somewhere."

I'd met up with Snowflake again. The Berlin rapper from

the MTV Awards. And he agreed with me, said, "Sure, you have your career."

Flakey was often in Hamburg and came to visit me. He always had some weed on him—the real reason we got together. At least, my reason.

We smoked some, just to relax. I could feel that it wasn't doing me much good. One time it brought the voices back. That wasn't funny. I kept this a secret from Kralle, as though she were my mother.

She found out, though.

Rosa was coming around again, probably had a bad conscience about how she'd cut me before. . . .

She shared a joint or two with us, and then she told on me to Kralle.

Kralle was hopping mad. "I'll never go to doctors with you again. Next time you fall apart I won't take care of you."

"I don't give a shit for your herbal teas and pills. X is a medication too."

I could feel myself getting worse, saying hurtful things like that. . . .

I started lying to the psycho-doctor, too. He said something about how being borderline caused my whole personality to be disturbed. "If you want to participate fully in life, you must make fundamental changes in yourself."

I acted like I was listening, but inwardly I laughed and thought, *Why don't you change? Quit being so uptight and boring!*

But what he said was mostly right. Helpful people were getting on my nerves. Most of all Kralle. I called her Florence Nightingale instead of thanking her for sticking by me when things got really bad and I was at my worst.

Of course, she wasn't always giving and caring. It happens in every relationship: Gradually the prince becomes a frog. Because you find out the unpleasant sides. But I was finding faults in her, instead of in myself.

Whatever she did, however she did it, she could do no right. I was tired of her everlasting herbal teas and noodle casseroles, and fed up with her constant chatter about how bad things were politically, socially, economically.

She'd pick the wrong moment to caress me, and I couldn't make her stop. She'd somehow always stroke my hair in the wrong direction. And she always got too close to me. It made me feel hemmed in, like she was trying to control me.

But . . . but it was worse when she left. Because then—and I'd just barely started to improve—my crazy jealousy came over me again.

At that time Kralle was friends with this woman, really butch—leather jacket, pugilist sports and all. When I knew they were together, I'd call Kralle every hour. Sometimes more often. Stupid of me, but I couldn't help it.

If I couldn't reach her, it drove me nearly insane. I felt deserted and betrayed, and I vividly pictured what she and that woman were doing. Like a movie of total despair.

The laughable thing about this was:

When I smoked pot with Flakey, I got hot.

He looked good naked, had cool upper arms and tattoos. Sad to say, it's easy to fool yourself into believing that good looks and steel-blue eyes with lightning in them make someone an interesting person. All he wanted afterward was to watch TV.

"Get out," I'd say.

I thought of the old joke—Magic trick: First we screw, then you vanish. I felt really cool. Like I'd kept the upper hand.

He split.

I stayed home alone, *I* watched TV. After a while, I tried to call Kralle. Couldn't reach her. Figured she was out with her pugilist lesbian. Got crazy jealous again.

Idiotic.

This woman came on to me, too. It was pretty long ago, before my thing with Kralle. Before Mira M. and the Spiders. I was in a bar, standing near the toilet, and suddenly she was behind me. We didn't know each other, but she grabbed my crotch from behind and whispered in my ear, "What's up, little one? Want to come with me?"

"Leave me alone."

"What an uncool slut you are," she said, and went on into the toilet.

In my jealousy fit I played and replayed this scene in my mind—but with that woman grabbing *Kralle's* crotch, saying, "Come with me." And Kralle *not* saying "Leave me alone," but following her into the toilet, and they undress, go at it . . .

None of that was real, I wasn't even sure they were

together someplace. But I experienced it live, in real time, with close-ups, in slow motion.

You can imagine the mood I was in when Kralle came over later that night. She let herself in. Had her own key. I didn't even say hello.

"Hey, what's wrong?" she asked. "Aren't you feeling well?"

I went out on the terrace to smoke.

She followed. "Sometimes it helps to talk about problems."

I felt too deeply aggrieved. When in fact it was *I* who'd cheated on *her*.

Man, I was supposed to be recovering. Making fundamental changes toward becoming a calm, reasonable person. "Someone who's in control of, not controlled by, her emotions," as the psychologist had said. Cool sentence.

That was out of the question now.

"At least be honest and admit it," was all I said after a long silence.

Kralle looked at me with her big, glowing eyes. I saw these eyes, and I loved them so much, it drove me berserk. But this one thing I couldn't do: I could not relent.

I wanted her to absolve herself, beg for forgiveness on her knees. Swear she'd never see that bitch again, never again turn off her cell phone.

This time I'd tried just once to reach her. And dropped calls do happen with cells. She might not even have turned hers off.

"I love you," was all she said.

"Love doesn't exist," I said. "Just self-love."

"I love you," she repeated.

"Then prove it."

If she hadn't started crying at that point, it might still have been all right. But she started to. And she asked, "What am I supposed to do for you? What can I still do?"

I went back inside, just like that, without a word. Somewhere in this big apartment OK kept a revolver. I had no idea anymore where it was. I tried the giant storage wall near the entrance. Started opening drawers. Kralle and I'd once tested it together.

A real revolver, with ammunition.

"You need a permit for it," Kralle'd said.

"OK must have one," I said.

Back then I'd loaded the cylinder with six cartridges and shot one from the terrace.

"Did I hit it?"

"Who? What?"

"The Elbe, silly."

"Yes. I think I heard her screaming. Listen."

We'd both listened hard, and really heard strange noises coming from the river. Probably a rusty crane. It sounded eerie.

Looking for that revolver now, I remembered that I'd put it someplace in the kitchen.

4. That Russian roulette thing really wasn't my own idea. I'd gotten it from watching Uncle Lou's roadies in Yugoland. They were hardboiled guys. One time they were playing—holding a revolver to someone's open hand, not to his temple. Once they held it to a mouse they'd caught. Each time they'd come up with a blank, they'd start over, spin the cylinder like a roulette wheel. It could take forever till they fired a shot.

It made a big impression on me. They'd aim at the spot on somebody's palm where the bullet presumably would go clean through without hitting a bone. They played two rounds and were lucky. Aiming at the mouse, they played as long as it took to kill it.

Not pretty.

But then not everything in life is pretty.

And now I thought: *Let's see if Kralle can stand this. And if I myself can stand it.* I thought: *If we're in earnest, if we really mean it, we'll do it.* And I realized I had to go first.

I searched through the drawers in the kitchen till Kralle came after me.

"What are you looking for?"

"This." I sat down at the kitchen table and took out the cartridges, all but one.

"What are you doing?"

I laid the revolver on the table with the cylinder open, so she could see the single cartridge still in it.

"If you really love me, prove it," I said.

I picked up the revolver, clicked the cylinder closed, spun it a few times. Then held the barrel to my temple.

Kralle stared at me.

"Stop with that shit!"

She raised her arm to grab my hand.

I said, "Don't. Or I'll pull the trigger."

She took her hand away, stayed sitting down.

The barrel felt cold, smelled metallic. I looked her in the eyes.

"I'm doing this for you," I said.

And pulled the trigger.

The click thundered like an explosion in my head.

I felt dizzy for a moment.

My hand started trembling. The thing was pretty heavy. . . . I laid it on the table and looked at her.

I was really pathetic.

"If you want me to believe you, then do it," I said.

Slid the revolver over to her.

She didn't take it. Looked at me, her eyes not beautiful then, just small and teary.

And she left.

She turned around once. I pretended not to look at her. The heavy door shut behind her. And I saw her on the video monitor going slowly down the broad stairs. I ran to the door but didn't open it. I watched her on the monitor gradually growing smaller, till she disappeared among the trees.

I kept looking at the monitor. Not because I counted on her reappearing. But because I was completely beside myself. I looked at the gray screen, on which the only things moving were branches of trees to the left and right of the stairs.

Later I stood on the terrace just as I was, no shoes on, and still—as though anesthetized. Then I went out, across the pebbled path, down the broad stairs to the Elbchaussee, and headed west, walking barefoot.

My feet were cold, which felt good. Sometimes I ran on tiptoe. People looked at me like I was crazy. But it was just a means to calm myself. To feel the earth.

What I want to say is: It didn't just hurt her. It hurt me, too. I never called Snowflake again. I'd score pot somewhere else.

A couple of weeks later I saw Kralle with someone new. Not the pugilist lesbo. I didn't care who.

It felt like a knife in my heart!

To get past it, I hurled myself back into working. It was time.

[TRACK 9]
FINAL COUNTDOWN

1. I'd taken three months off. Why let myself in for all the craziness again? At our first concert I knew why. It was in the Hamburg market hall, a medium-size shed, the perfect place for a fantastic gig. We came back out after the first set to wild applause, everybody yelling, "Encore! Encore!" Along with that, the blinding lights, the hot, moist air, the amplifiers humming when Giorgio turned the volume up. Oh yes, I knew why: This was like taking off into space and landing back on Earth, triumphant. It was worth it, worth everything. . . . Standing at the mike, with the band behind you, and it all works, everyone doing his thing, not needing to look at one another, it was as though you're one great, enormous instrument, being played by someone else. And then a sing-along—so what if the lyrics are really dumb? Everybody's singing, loud, and the people in the first row stretch their hands out, try to touch you. . . .

It's only rock 'n' roll—but I like it.

We went to the studio again. Began rehearsing, or rather, tried out new songs, recorded our early versions.

When I was asked, I'd always answered, "Yes, I'm still writing songs"—and I was. Now we badly needed new material, for concerts, but even more urgently for a new single,

then for an album, and soon. But the truth was, the things I'd
been writing weren't really finished. Here and there a nice
verse, but with no fitting refrain; or a cool refrain, but no real
song. Just flashes of ideas.

If the pressure with the first album was great, now it
was unbearable. Everyone said the second album is the big
stumbling block. Only very few bands succeed with it. Even
superstars like the Stones had their second album flop. If the
first was a big hit, everyone expected you to outdo yourself.
Not that easy! OK kept asking, "Does every song have a great
hook line? Is it right for radio?"

Clearly, that's how a song has to be.

But I'd written the old numbers for myself. Because I just
felt like it. Or because I needed to work something out. I'd
meant those old songs to be private. For me. To sing to myself
alone, and maybe to a few good friends.

These new songs had to be for marketing, items to be sold.

When I sat looking at scraps of paper I'd scribbled text
lines and chords on, I sometimes felt as though these notes
were looking back at me, saying, *What are you doing to us? Mira,
don't give us away. We belong only to you.*

I tried to ignore that. We needed new material. It had to be
good. And for that you have to use your most personal, most
intimate ideas. Those are the best.

Those old songs—I never even took them seriously.
"Famous," that one just came from being drunk, or maybe high.
I realized only now, when I needed to come up with twelve
new ones, those old songs were pretty good. . . .

+   +   +

The whole music business had the jitters; profits were down,
partly due to Internet pirating; the marketing people were
shitting their pants. Bringing out an album isn't cheap, you have
to figure on a few hundred thousand euro just for packaging,
the booklet, promotion and advertising, and on top of that,
studio costs, production, etc.

Then too, the concerts canceled when I was sick had cost
OK a bunch of money. Besides, nobody even knew if people
still wanted an album from Mira M.

OK explained all that to me. Tastes got more and more
faddish, and their life spans ever shorter. What can happen is,
today's kids turn up their noses at yesterday's top-selling band,
declare it totally uncool.

The recording company balked at making an advance video,
wanted the single to be the trial balloon to see how the
radio stations would react. And I knew: If it doesn't get played,
there'll be no album, no new contract, no tour, so we'll play in
the boondocks for a hundred euros a night like two years ago
and be the has-beens who'd never really made it.

And then I'll be through with EOK Productions. No more
apartment. Just like it was for Melody. Pack up my stuff and
get out.

But at least I had a personal manager: Rosa. That was good.
OK had arranged it.

As I said, we'd become closer again, she came over

sometimes. But Melody mustn't know, or she'd give Rosa hell.

Melo had swallowed her pride and was staying at Rosa's. But there was tension between them. From sharing close quarters. And because Rosa realized what Melo was putting me through about "Famous."

This was after Melo had hired a lawyer. And appeared on that talk show, and openly bad-mouthed me. Burst into tears right in front of the camera. Said things that everybody knew were idiotic.

Rosa and Zucka both thought she'd gone too far. The day of that talk show, Rosa came over and said, "I was against her doing it. I tried to persuade her not to."

I let Rosa hear Melo's message on my cell phone—to laugh or cry about? The one of Melo threatening that she would make "two further revelations" about me.

What happened to Melo can happen to anyone who's focused on hatred. That's what I learned. She went on and on about it to Rosa, until Rosa couldn't listen to it anymore.

She asked Rosa to stop being friends with me. When Rosa refused, Melody accused her of treachery, said the whole thing was an intrigue and that Rosa had carefully plotted it. How? By going to OK, discrediting Melo, telling him what a state she was in.

So now, all of a sudden, it wasn't just Mira who'd lied and been false, but also Rosa.

That's why Rosa started coming to see me again, and even asked me to forgive her. But something between us had changed. No, it was actually something in me. Something that had *not* changed. It was the same old thing: my not trusting people. Not even Rosa, at least not 100 percent.

Which brings us back to the apartment.

[TRACK 10]
JANUARY 14, 2004:
PART FOUR

1. Trust people? Rosa sat in the orange swivel chair and wondered, empty-eyed, *How can you really trust anyone?*

She looked at Melody, who so liked gazing out at the Elbe, the container harbor, the Kohlbrand bridge. At Kralle, sitting, lips pressed together, at the large table. At Zucka, busy sorting the cell phones again, and still in love with Melody, although officially he now was with her, Rosa—for financial reasons, as she said (meaning he was broke and she helped him out).

They'd been together for five or six hours, on this anniversary of the stowaways' landing in Hamburg seven years ago.

Fried sweet potatoes and banku and Kralle's lasagna. And Rosa had made dessert. Like every year. Other than that, nothing was as before. Because Mira was no longer there.

And because something had changed in this vast, too sparsely furnished apartment. It was as though the smell of death hung in the air.

Whenever Rosa looked at the aquarium, this picture came before her eyes: transparent clouds of blood reddening the greenish water; strands of Mira's black hair moving upward with the rising air bubbles; and Mira, facedown, as though searching for something at the bottom.

Rosa remembered the puddles on the floor, and struggling to lift Mira out . . .

Even though Mira had lost a lot of weight in those last months.

Her slender body was as cold as the water. But her face looked relaxed, her mouth seemed to smile, as though wanting to say, *It's all behind me now.*

Rosa's brain again refused to believe what had happened. Only a short while before, she and Mira had stood in OK's office, waiting for the latest charts to come up on the computer screen. Mira saying something. Laughing.

A person can't just suddenly be gone. . . .

Nevertheless, now Zucka was sorting out that person's cell phones. Rosa wondered how many more he would find. He lined them up by model on the windowsill, among the pistachio shells.

Kralle sat at the large gray table in her blue pinstripe suit and red and white shoes. A good costume to hide her pain behind, Rosa thought. And still all those silver rings on her fingers . . .

Melo, as usual, stood at the window, looking out at the terrace.

To stop reproaching one another—good idea. Even better would be if they had other things to talk or think about instead. Looking at Kralle, Rosa knew that Kralle had scored speed for Mira. And had left her in the end, for someone else.

And looking at Melody, Rosa remembered that atrocious talk show, and Melody revealing the "truth"—that Mira M. did not write her own songs, no, that she'd stolen them from her best friend.

And when she looked again at Zucka . . .

Zucka now stood at the aquarium. Looking at the fish.

"Hey, Zucka. Say something," Rosa said.

"Like what?"

"Doesn't matter."

Zucka bent down, tapped at the glass pane, scared the fish. Then he asked, "Do they actually have sex?"

"The fish?" Rosa asked.

"Nah," Kralle said.

"So how do they make children?" Rosa asked.

"The females lay down roe for the males to squirt on."

"Boring," said Zucka.

"One kind does have sex," Melody said, turning toward them.

"Seriously?"

"Yes, the mouthbreeders. They carry their eggs in their mouths. The little males come sneaking over on the sly, and when the females open up their mouths, they stick their tails in, quick, and squirt away."

When no one said anything, Melody added, "I know that from biology class."

"Fascinating," Rosa said. "I think I'll do the dishes. Who wants to help?"

"I'll be right there," said Zucka.

Rosa went into the kitchen, ran the hot water, gave it a spritz of detergent. Tiny white foam bubbles like fish roe floated toward her.

2. Fish and sex. Why not? What else was there to talk about?

Rosa thought about Thursdays—standing around with everybody in the studio, watching the Media Control Charts website, to see if Mira's new single had made it into the top one hundred.

It either happens in the first few weeks or never, they all knew.

To sell well, you first had to be on the charts. Or else no go. And you had to sell really big. A label like EOK Productions was an independent venture. OK had invested his own dough—a lot. So then, if Mira flopped . . .

The radio people's reaction was less than euphoric; they didn't play the new song much except in Hamburg and Berlin.

Mira had worn her sunglasses all day, and Rosa knew why: so no one could see how exhausted she looked. And how insecure . . .

Rosa shook her head. Again she saw Mira's face the way it was when she'd found her—mute, smiling, cold, dead.

"Farewell" was Mira's last song.

I'm not where I started from
So where am I?

Every night, another party
Sometime, every party ends.

Cool song. And it didn't flop. Rosa remembered the Thursday, everyone sitting around the computer, when the first announcement came. They could have gotten the news on e-mail, but the website was quicker. The band had done a few promo gigs that week, and now they were in seventy-fourth place. Starting from zero.

Rosa sniffled, started stacking plates beside the sink.

OK had said, "Street but sweet," that Mira was the real thing, tough enough to be believed and sweet enough to get through to the media.

Rosa dried her hands and flipped her cell phone open. She hadn't deleted that last text message: "Till tomorrow. :-) Mira."

The night before that "tomorrow," when Rosa had entered the apartment, Mira was clutching ice cubes in her hands. Rosa touched them and got scared. Mira's fingers were freezing.

Probably also from doing speed, Rosa had thought. The girl was a time bomb, set to detonate, who knew when? Next day, with the next dose? Mira's heart was racing, Rosa guessed . . . Most likely from fear, and the voices were back . . .

+   +   +

"Am I supposed to do all the dishes by myself?" Rosa put her cell phone away.

Kralle didn't answer, just looked anxious and bewildered.

"Be right there," Zucka said, lighting a cigarette.

Melody sighed, stood up. "Okay . . ."

She came into the kitchen. Rosa tossed her a dish towel, pointed to the stack of plates and to one of the cabinets.

Melody said, "I know which cabinet they go in. I lived here, remember?"

3. Zucka laid the cigarette in the ashtray. From the kitchen he heard the clatter of plates and Rosa's and Melo's voices. He went to the storage wall near the entrance door.

In one of the drawers there Rosa had stowed the box of minicassettes for the recorder when she and he had been alone in the apartment.

If anyone had asked me, I wouldn't have guessed that Zucka was still going to play a decisive role in this story.

Like I said, he always had this stupid grin on, from smoking all that pot, and so I'd underestimated him, and didn't grasp that there was one thing he was seriously interested in, and that was honesty.

Because Zucka's ghetto, not one of slums, consisted of elegant houses—and of lies.

Possibly he understood quite a bit more than I'd given him credit for.

I watched him at the storage wall, opening drawers, looking for the box of cassettes.

And here's the kicker: I know of course which song I
wrote and which I did not. But this box, I have to admit,
contained one cassette with "Melo" written on it. In Melo's
handwriting. One cassette—she'd recorded when she still
lived here—she now was desperate to find. And this was
the cassette that Zucka took out, looked at, turned over. On
the reverse side was written, barely legibly: "Don't Wanna Be
Famous."

He noticed, while still standing there, that somebody had
come up behind him.

"What are you doing?" Kralle asked.

"Nothin'," Zucka said.

"Yes, something."

Zucka slid the "Melo" cassette into his pants pocket. Then,
pointing to the cassettes in the box, "They're all blank, nothing
on them."

He looked at Kralle.

She sank down to the small blue rug by the entrance door.
She motioned toward the kitchen, said, "I can't."

"Can't what?"

"Help wash up."

"I don't want to either," Zucka said.

"It's not that I mind doing dishes." She leaned back and
closed her big green eyes. "It's because the kitchen is where
she handed me the revolver."

Zucka nodded, sat. "Rosa told me about that."

"Yes. And now people are saying it's my fault she OD'd and
all. What crap."

"Right."

"I saw how she pulled away from me. And that she needed me more than ever. But I just couldn't bear it."

Kralle turned to Zucka, her face distorted like in a hollow mirror, her body crumpling, and tears filling her eyes.

And me, I had to look on, watch all this . . .

Hey, Kralle!

Listen: There's no reason to cry. Really, none!

Kralle, I was just so scared. A little rabbit, too scared to crawl out of its burrow.

In any case, no reason to cry.

It's no one's fault. If anyone's to blame, it's me.

And that stupid eel.

Kralle let herself slump sideways, leaned against Zucka. Till he put his arms around her.

4. "Come on now." Zucka stood, got her a handkerchief. She blew her nose and wiped her face.

They sat side by side, silent awhile.

Then he asked, "Do you really plan to write something about her?"

"I ask myself that question too," Kralle said. "I keep wondering, is it right? Although she wanted me to. She said to me once, 'When I'm not here anymore, write everything down.'"

"Everything? You think you know the truth of everything?"

"Truth?" Kralle asked. "What is that?" She blew her nose

again. "You can never write what's actual," she said. "Only dreams."

Zucka pointed to the aquarium. "Did you know that fish don't dream? They're the only quite evolved creatures that don't."

"Is that so?"

"Yes, because they don't sleep. Or they do, but always just with half their brain. The other half stays awake. So they don't drown."

"Drown? Fish?"

"They can. Because they also have to breathe."

He stood up and rummaged in his pants pocket.

"If you really want to write something—maybe you can use this." He took out the cassette. "Rosa hid it. Didn't want me to hear it."

"What is it?"

"It has Melo's name on it."

Zucka glanced toward the kitchen. He heard the clatter of silverware being put away. "Here, Kralle." He held out the cassette.

Kralle took it and held it close to her eyes, as if she were nearsighted. "'Melo.'" Turned it over. "'Don't Wanna Be Famous.' What *is* this?"

"The cassette she's been frantic to find. The real reason why she came tonight."

Kralle scratched her forehead. "Yes, she mentioned such a thing to me."

"She mentioned it to everyone, I think."

"And why don't you give it to her?"

Zucka just shrugged his shoulders.

At this moment Melody appeared from the passageway to the kitchen. "I think this is really uncool," she said. "I did my share, now it's your turn."

Kralle turned halfway around. "We're coming."

"Yes, but when?"

Kralle very calmly started pulling on the tape. She kept pulling, and with one quick motion ripped it out. Then she bunched it all up, set it down on the stone floor.

Melody came nearer. "What's that?"

"Some kind of tape that Zucka found," Kralle said. She took out her lighter and held it to the tape, saying under her breath, as though to herself, "Speak now. Or forever hold your peace."

At first the tape didn't catch fire, then suddenly it burst into a tongue of flame.

"What are you doing?" Melo came over to them. "Zucka, was this something of yours?"

The empty cassette lay on the floor next to Kralle. Melody bent down and took it, studied what was written on it—for a long time, as though it were pretty hard reading all that.

Finally she said, "It says 'Melo' . . ." She stared at the melted little heap on the floor. "Listen . . . Zucka?"

Zucka moved his hands, warded her off.

"That's *mine*!"

Kralle gave her a blank stare. "Too bad . . . too late."

+   +   +

Rosa had come out of the kitchen.

"What's going on?"

Then the telephone rang.

[TRACK 11]
THE TRUTH ABOUT MIRA M.

1. I know which song I wrote. That one. I wrote it.

But I admit, there really was this cassette with "Melo" on it. And on the reverse side, very faintly, in ballpoint pen, "Don't Wanna Be Famous."

No one knows what was on that tape. It lay half burnt, half melted on the stone tiles in front of the entrance to the big apartment.

Too bad.

I know I wrote that song. I even know where and when I wrote it: sitting in Kralle's pothead flat after meeting with OK that first time when he blew off our demo tape. I thought of Melo while I wrote it. Melo in a sexy glitter costume, standing on disco stages, trilling techno songs. Melody, who meantime had been hearing voices and probably was in a psycho ward.

And I thought: I don't want that to be me. That kind of wannabe star. I don't wanna be a wannabe . . .

That was the first line I thought of: "I don't wanna be a wannabe superstar. . . ."

That was all that came to me. I couldn't think of more right then. Because I was still so pissed off at that fat cat OK, sitting behind his fat EOK desk, interlacing his fat fingers and explaining that a demo tape mustn't be too long. . . .

I leaned back, thought about nothing, smoked. And
suddenly I got inspired, finished the song in a quarter of an
hour. Or anyway, the main idea. "Don't Wanna Be Famous."

I knew that I had written it.

But what does one really know?

The first thing you realize up here is that down there you
don't know anything. Being down there and really knowing
something—not possible. One precludes the other.

It's pretty nice, being down there. But everything's illusion.
And ultimately leads to disillusion. Which hurts. But you see
clearly. More clearly, anyway.

Which doesn't mean that you're all-knowing up here.

I wasn't able to reconstruct what really was on that tape.
Zucka had found it and not even he knew, because he hadn't
gotten around to listening to it. Because Rosa had snatched it
away.

"That's none of your business," she said.

"No?" asked Zucka.

"No."

It's strange. Sometimes I feel I *do* remember, dimly, very
fleetingly: Melo talking to me about her song ideas. Back when
she lived in the apartment. I'd slept over. She came home early
in the morning, totally wired from her shows. And I heard—
at least I *think* I heard—her sing: "Don't wanna be famous."
Not the whole stanza, just these two lines: "Don't wanna be
famous/Don't wanna be a star . . ."

Different melody, different phrasing. Wannabe R & B style.
But those two lines—it's possible that she sang them to me.

I can't tell. Is it a genuine memory? Or just the residue
of her persistent propaganda? *She'd* created that song—she
said that to me over and over, maybe a hundred times, with
variations on just when and where she'd told me the idea. It
was sheer brainwashing.

What I now remembered was one variation. Because there
was this tape she'd wanted so desperately to find, believing it
would be proof.

It's like what somebody once said to me: Every really
good idea was worked on by different persons at different
times, without any of these persons knowing about the others.
Maybe that's what happened with the song. That we both had
the idea.

2. But one thing I do know, that others can only wonder about:
Exactly how I died.

It really was an accident. And it was no one's "fault." Except
possibly the eel's. How you die is accidental. Anyway, that's
how it was for me. Death is unavoidable, but you can't foresee
it. Except if you're an old, wise yogi.

Or if you commit suicide.

Which, as I said, I did not.

It was carelessness. I absolutely had to retrieve that stupid
cell phone I'd dropped. And I was tired. Not just tired in my
body but in my mind from the stress. Sometimes I thought
about being left in peace at last, lying dead in a cool grave,

no appointments, phone calls, tour buses, interviews, crazed teenage fans. . . .

And suddenly I lay in this aquarium. Everything went black. My mouth and nose were underwater, I couldn't get air anymore. Soon my brain ran out of oxygen, switched itself off. I was unconscious. . . .

And it was a nice day.

Oddly, already that morning I'd had a sense that something was going to end. Not my whole life—I had no such premonition. Just that a part of it was over.

And it made me sentimental. Because I was a sentimental person.

That's how I got the idea to visit Uncle Lou. When I was still going to school, we sometimes ran into each other. And when Oma died he and I drove to Yugoland together. And then, after not seeing him for a really long time, I saw him again, at a concert a few weeks back. Some concert, I don't even know where. Someplace in southern Germany.

We'd just finished our sound check. This rock 'n' roll group was scheduled to play before us, a real one, old guys with long hair like manes. And when they came onstage to do their own sound check, I couldn't believe my eyes. The guy with the guitar, none other than Uncle Lou!

I dashed over to him, threw my arms around his neck.

There wasn't much time before his group was announced, and then ours. And after that we had to rush off to the next tour dates.

Anyway, now I had an urge to go see Uncle Lou again.
Maybe to get some good vibes off him. He'd been supernice to
me before that concert.

Man, this tough-minded old pro told me: "I admire you."

He had this wonderful Yugoslav accent. The one I'd forced
myself to lose. It made me feel at home.

"Hey, Lou, I admire *you!*"

He brushed that aside. Said, "Mira, I mean it. Because you
stick with what's really your thing. Not me. I never did. I always
did what was commercial. Played guitar for other people, for
dough. And now look at me. I'm sixty and still have to tour."

I wanted to see him again and have more time. So I got into
my Smart Cabrio and drove straight to the little house from
years ago.

Funny that a guy like this lived in a standard little row
house, just like the countless other little houses you go past,
driving to Buchholz in the Nordheide.

I parked but stayed in the car. I couldn't tell if anyone was
home. And I didn't know if he still had the same girlfriend
(whom I was allowed to call "Aunt").

I didn't dare go ring the bell. What would I say? I thought
about how I'd split, taken off with my sleeping bag, savings
book, and their hundred mark. Lou must have worried at the
time, and been plenty pissed off....

I saw no light on in the house, but why would there have
been, during the day? Sometimes it looked as though someone
was moving behind the half-drawn shades, but I couldn't be sure.

I sat in the car quite a while, smoked, listened to a couple

of CDs. Gazed at this little house that once was my home—
for how long? Let's see. Four or five years ... The only place
where I'd stayed that long.

What would I have done if Lou had come out right then?
Stayed in the car? Or driven off? Or run to him? I don't know.

Avoiding things was not my style. But meeting up with him
earlier had been so nice. ... I didn't want to ruin that by seeing
him hung over, still in his bathrobe, sleepy, and in a rotten mood.

I thought of my parents. I never missed them. Hadn't seen
them in a long time, not since Oma's funeral.

I hardly even understood their language anymore. And
anyway, the world I grew up in had vanished. Yugoland didn't
exist anymore. Now there was just Croatia and Slovenia and
Serbia and so on.

Anyway, I felt closer to Uncle Lou.

Nothing stirred in there, he clearly wasn't home. But just in
case he was, I couldn't ring the doorbell now. Because then I'd
have had to stay a few hours, which I didn't have to spare. So I
drove away.

It was a strange day. I asked myself what I would have had of
life if it were ending now.

And I answered: All sorts of things. I told myself: *You actually
could feel quite satisfied.*

Next week, concerts in Austria and Bavaria.

My career wasn't over. "Farewell" hadn't become a number
one hit, but it made the charts all the same. My career
continued as before. Went well, was even fun.

It was just strange, this feeling I had. Like that night at the
MTV awards, that great show in Barcelona ... feeling like I
wasn't really present, that everything was happening without
me ...

Since then I'd felt like this pretty often onstage. I'd stand at
the mike, but also next to myself, observing.

True, I'd snorted speed.

On tour during that insanely hot summer of 2003, we'd
played dozens of outdoor festivals. And the album came out
that fall. And didn't flop—on the contrary. And we kept on
touring.

I guess I'd been long-range stoned since New Year's. Worst
thing about a speed OD is the tingly feeling, like a thousand
ants are crawling around in your head. It makes you crazy. You
have to scratch all the time and chain-smoke cigarettes.

No, even worse is how your heart keeps racing, and the
fear that it will never stop.

But then it does. Like when a raging storm abates.

In the evening I called Rosa.

That was important. Like leaping over my shadow, calling
someone, asking for help. Saying: I'm scared, I don't feel
well. Would you come over?

Rosa came. She couldn't help me. But at least I wasn't alone.
I threw up, and she held me.

And then we talked about all kinds of things.

Some time or other I fell asleep.

+   +   +

3. Later I sat on the terrace half the night. The cold feels good to someone diagnosed with "undifferentiated psychotic disturbance." Just pleasantly cool. Things came into focus, had contours again. I was less dizzy, stopped needing to throw up.

I looked at the stars in the winter night. Thought: *This is my TV. I sit here and my favorite show is on. No cost, no electronic smog.* "The Stars. Brought to you live."

And it wasn't from the drugs. Just a natural high.

Gradually it grew light. I watched trucks, small as toy cars, creeping over the Kohlbrand bridge in slow motion. And I asked myself why objects in the distance seem to move so sluggishly.

Then I remembered something.

The place I'd found, back when I was a child.

The other children had gone ahead. I kept sitting on the grass and looked around. The trees, light glinting through the leaves, the hills . . . I felt contented in this place. Although it was just a junkyard. I said to myself, *You don't need more.* And then I found the big tire, and I could climb into it and sit. The man in the truck couldn't see me sitting there. Nor could anybody else. No one knew about this hiding place. I lived there in my own world.

I knew that I'd discovered something. Something I could never lose.

I thought of that while sitting on the terrace. And then of Jackson. Who never could understand me, and whom I could never understand. The great love that comes only once. I'd asked myself so many times why he'd left, gone back

to Ghana. And now I understood: He'd felt that in Germany
something inside him was being destroyed.

That's why he'd gone.

4. And I thought of Rosa. I wanted to text-message her. Just
quickly: "Till tomorrow. :-) Mira."

I went back inside, got my cell phone. Leaned against the
aquarium, talked to the fish. But not because I was crazy.
Everyone talks to pets sometimes. I didn't have any others.

I reached into the fodder-fish tank, grabbed a few of those
poor little creatures, and tossed them in for the sturgeons.
Sturgeons always swim on top. The eel, also nocturnal, glared
at me in a funny way.

I took it as a reproach and said, "Okay, I'll take you out, just
like I promised."

I text-messaged Rosa, got unnerved, kept making typos,
sent it off anyway.

I bent over the water, puffed air at the fish.

I always felt sorry for those little fodder fish. They came
into the aquarium, the big world for them, just to be eaten up.
Hmm. Tragic.

Then the cell slipped out of my other hand and fell into the
water.

I reached for it right away but couldn't grab hold.

I watched it through the thick glass, slowly drifting down.

First I thought, *Just leave it there, Mira. It's probably ruined,
and you have enough others.* But all my addresses were on it.
I tried to fish it out, but it was all the way down in the algae.

I couldn't reach that far, my arm was too short.

I wondered if Rosa would still get the text message. Oh well, it wasn't that important.

But the addresses were important.

That's why I stripped down to my T-shirt and brought over a chair to stand on. "Don't be afraid," I told the fish. "I won't do anything to you. I'll quickly get out." I just wanted to retrieve the cell phone. I let myself slowly glide into the water.

It startled me how cold it was.

I took a gulp of air, closed my mouth, and dived under.

Just then I felt the burning pain in my hand.

I'd kept my eyes open to look for the phone. And now I saw that the eel had bitten into my hand. *Mean, ungrateful beast,* I thought, resurfacing. *You feed him months on end, and then...*

The blood dripped into the water, formed a fine, transparent cloud. I glanced at the eel and considered, should I dive down again? I searched for the cell. There... no.

I dived down but couldn't see it. Didn't see anything anymore. Not the green algae, not the brightly colored little fish, not the eel.

Nothing but blackness before my eyes.

I lost consciousness.

And then I was gone.

[TRACK 12]
JANUARY 14, 2004:
THE FINAL PART

1. The telephone rang.

Melody turned to Rosa. "That's mine!" she said.

Zucka slowly pulled himself up from the blue rug he'd been sitting on.

Kralle squatted in front of the little heap of melted tape on the stone tile floor.

Melo stood next to her, studying the empty cassette.

The telephone kept ringing.

They all looked around as though they couldn't understand where the sound was coming from. Nobody moved.

At last Rosa picked up.

"Hello? Yes, I was just busy in the kitchen." She turned to the others and leaned against the tabletop. "Yes, so far."

She put the receiver down on the table, motioned to Zucka. "It's your papa."

Zucka went and took the phone.

"Hey, Papa. Yes, fine. And you?"

Then he said, "Yes, she's here. You know, it's our get-together. Like every year." He nodded. "Yes, obviously."

He went to Melody.

"For you." He handed her the phone.

But it was a while before she said a single word.

"Yes . . ."

Then, as she listened, her face slowly changed, opened.

"I know. Yes, I know. Yes? Really?"

Now she was ready to have a conversation. You could tell by her tone of voice. Not icy anymore.

"Right. But . . . Right. Yes, with pleasure. Honestly, I . . ."

2. Honestly, I figured this might happen:

OK taking up again with the girl he'd dropped a year and a half ago.

The great producer getting in touch.

Melody kept saying the same thing. "Yes, right, why not . . . Yes, naturally. I'd like to! Yes . . ."

I knew how he operated.

And what he'd called about.

He'd showed me the material, asked, Wasn't there something there for me? Because if so, we could bring out another album. . . .

It wasn't so bad, but not right for Mira M. and the Spiders. More like the stuff he'd made with Melody. Although he said, "It's a brand-new idea."

No, basically the same old stuff. A little more ambiance— harmonic, not so techno, plus a little rock guitar—but really not for me.

I'd wondered when he'd offer it to Melo. And she'd snap it up, I figured.

Melody had never told me what the voices she'd heard

had been saying. Apparently they'd spurred her on: Never give up. That was Melo's motto: It doesn't matter how often you fall on your face. Just that you get up again.

Unless you're dead.

And so it happened that a few days later Melody sat in the comfortable black swivel chair again in front of OK's big desk.

Where at first they chattered about old times.

Reminisced about shared successes.

About Luisa. Luisa, now called Melody, also Mel'O.

Soon to be called BTB, which stood for "Blood Thirsty Babe." OK's new project. Lounge music, he called it. "Techno, that's over. And nu-rock, too. Now people want something smooth, with just the right lovely voice. Like yours . . ."

Melody was all smiles. Said yes to everything.

Every human, after all, longs to be somebody interesting, somebody who matters. And if you have to go by a new name and wear stupid-looking costumes for appearances on disco stages or afternoon talk shows, it's really not too high a price to pay. And Melody knew it.

[LAST TRACK]
JACKSON'S DREAM

1. On the night when Mira's cell phone fell into the aquarium . . .

When she tried to retrieve it, and the eel bit her, which caused her to lose consciousness . . .

And the oxygen supply to her brain gave out . . .

That night, in Tema, southern Ghana, Jackson had a dream.

He'd smoked one more cigarette, closed the door of the shed that housed his video theater, and rolled out his mat in front of the screen.

And as often happened, his mind's eye saw images from the films he'd shown—usually one or two from America and one from Africa.

That evening one film he'd shown was about a man who sold tropical fish, smuggling them into the United States for lots of money.

When he'd first seen that film, Jackson thought of the apartment Melody had moved into just around that time. Thought of the giant aquarium with the motionless fish. Then he'd had a dream about Mira.

Jackson knew that she had moved in after Melo. Mira wrote to him every few months, kept him informed. But he hadn't imagined how things were.

And now he dreamed of her.

He saw her, but instead of being Mira she was a colorful fish. She had many friends, but they were all fish too. They had pointy teeth, and they ate Mira's face.

Jackson woke up in the middle of the hot, humid night. He listened to the sounds of mosquitoes and frogs.

He couldn't get back to sleep. Not even after taking a sip of water, after going outside and smoking another cigarette.

He lay back down on his mat. And thought about how he might return to Germany.

He knew he'd never travel inside a container again.

He knew lots of people who now lived "upstairs," which meant in Europe. Most of them had gone the land route through West Africa and Morocco, then crossed over to Spain.

That was cheaper and supposedly less dangerous.

Jackson thought of the sturgeons, and then of the eel . . .

The fish had eaten her face . . .

He found a job on a ship, working in the torrid engine rooms.

His plan was to sneak ashore at the first German port and somehow get to Hamburg.

Fourteen days later he was in Rostock.

At the port, on the first magazine kiosk, he saw Mira's picture. Her picture was on all the front pages. Mira M.

Jackson knew hardly any German anymore. He'd quickly forgotten what little he'd learned. But seeing her face on all the papers, he knew he'd arrived too late.

He stood at the kiosk at the port of Rostock and puzzled out the headlines, word for word:

SHE SANG ABOUT FREEDOM AND LOVE AND ENDED IN AN AQUARIUM. DEAD POP STAR: HER OLD FRIENDS SPEAK.

When he looked closer, he recognized a little photo next to Mira's: Of Luisa, now called Melody, and soon to be BTB—for "Blood Thirsty Babe."

Jackson reboarded the ship. Gave up on Hamburg. But he bought every paper that had Mira's photo on it.

The saleswoman also showed him a DVD: "Crazy Diamond: The Rise and Fall of Mira M. and the Spiders from Venus."

And a big poster.

Months later, when Jackson landed again in Tema, in southern Ghana, he had a DVD player and a new video projector in his luggage. He'd spent his entire pay on those.

Jackson took the bus to his small suburb. Went to the video-theater shed. Next day he changed the big sign from JACKSON'S VIDEO THEATER to JACKSON'S DVD CLUB.

The reopening took place that night.

And on that night, after the regular program, Jackson

showed the DVD he'd bought in Rostock—"Crazy Diamond: The Rise and Fall of Mira M. and the Spiders from Venus."

The DVD was in German, but no matter. Hardly anyone stayed to see it.

Jackson didn't care. From then on he showed it at the end of every evening.

[EXTRA HIDDEN BONUS TRACK] FAMOUS LAST WORDS

1. Why does a person commit suicide?

I can't say exactly. After all, I never did. Probably for a variety of reasons. I can only say why I came close a couple of times. Essentially it was despair, to do with love, no-longer-love.

I can only say how it felt. As black as when I woke up inside Uncle Lou's amp case. So dark I couldn't see a thing, not even my own hand before my eyes. I was locked in and alone, not knowing where I was, who I was, or anything.

Buried alive, but by my own life, by unhappiness that I made myself.

Unhappiness is always with us, but sometimes you can fool yourself by pretending it's not. Then something goes awry, and somebody stops loving you. And then it gets so bad, you can't stand it anymore.

And you think: *If I were gone now, no longer alive—then this burning unhappiness would be gone too. Also love's misery, hurt, disappointment, all that shit.*

If I were gone—no more pain. At moments like that I would think, *Just make an end.*

But then you still don't do it. Why not, I don't know.

I think one thing is clear. Either misery rolls over you the first time and you hurl yourself down off life's cliff when you're still a child. Or misery engulfs you again and again, for years, till one day you decide that's it, enough.

And then we kill ourselves. We may not commit suicide. But we kill something inside ourselves. So as not to keep on feeling pain.

That is the reason people start to harden. Something we've killed in ourselves turns hard. You see it in faces that sometimes grow as hard as masks you no longer can take off.

It's obvious, Kralle. Yes, of course people wear masks. I watched you at my funeral, and I know—don't know how, I just do—what you were thinking: That those people aren't honest, least of all with themselves. And you felt like ripping their masks off. But one mustn't, just like that.

2. At the school I went to while I lived at Uncle Lou's, we once put plaster-of-Paris strips on our faces. It was an art project: making masks. I'd signed up for it because I was being a good little girl and trying to have friends. I thought I'd meet nice friends that way. Oh, I'll never forget that art room. . . .

An older student was in charge. But the student who helped me with my plaster strips forgot to first smear on Vaseline. She stuck the damp strips right on my skin. It felt pretty bad, but I thought I shouldn't say anything, because I wanted to behave well. Besides, I still had this accent back then, so I often kept quiet.

When the plaster started to harden, my skin pulled together, felt stretched tight, but I thought it was supposed to. It took forever to dry out and harden. We all lay there so long, it was like we were meditating. I stared at the ceiling. That was pleasant, because finally my face felt nice and warm, and I was able to relax.

Then the masks had to come off. For a few of us this wasn't easy. For me, impossible. Because of no Vaseline. The student who'd forgotten to smear it on started trying to remove the mask, first carefully, then she tore at it, hard. It hurt like hell. And the mask wouldn't come off.

After a while the student in charge came over. And the two of them yanked on my mask—I thought they were skinning me alive. Finally a bit of it came loose at the edge. I screamed with pain, but they kept tugging. Larger and larger pieces came loose. And each piece felt like a part of my face tearing off.

I believe this is exactly how people must feel when the hardened masks they've worn for years are torn off. And Kralle, this is why one must be careful.

Maybe, Kralle, you believe that writers have a duty to tear masks off, show what people are really like. But isn't believing this also a mask? A writer's mask, but not so different from others'?

3. When I was in the clinic, after the MTV Awards, after Barcelona . . .

After the voices had begun and I slowly learned how to deal with them . . .

In the psych clinic, in this big brick building that looked like some stately English home . . .

I often took walks in the park with old trees. When the

sun shone. One time I stopped under a great beech tree, when the sun stood quite low, and the grass...

The sun stood low and shone diagonally across the grass. The leafy branches of the trees shaded my face, and I could see that all the grass, the entire meadow was covered with cobwebs, fine cobwebs vibrating with the stirring of the air.

And I could see them because the sun stood so low and caught itself in their laciness. And I remembered that I'd seen this before, when I was a child and sat in the junkyard, among the rusted auto parts.

It was as though the entire ground was covered by a net, almost like a cocoon. A wide-mesh net, because the spaces between the threads were pretty big, but still a net. Only you normally don't see it, because the sunlight doesn't break up in it.

You only see it when the sun stands very low. And even then you may not see it, if the sun is blinding.

But at that moment, standing under the big tree, I could see them, the gossamer threads on the grass. And I thought: This net is always there, like dust that you sometimes see in a sunbeam, but the dust is always there, of course. You pass by this net without noticing it; and only in this special light do you see it.

I asked myself, *How can there be so very many spiders, and where do they get so very, very many threads to cover this whole big meadow?*

And when I looked more closely, I noticed that the cobwebs were also right here where I stood, under the tree, interlaced with the few grass blades growing in this spot. And it became clear to me that probably the whole world is covered by a finely spun net that lies over it like a cloth. This cloth is spread over the whole world, but we don't see it.

And as I walked back to the building, then I knew: With every step I take, I tread on cobwebs and I tear them.

AFTERWORD AND ACKNOWLEDGMENTS

This is a novel, a story from my fantasies.

But it's also more, and has its own origin. It would not have been possible without the collaboration of numerous young actors, rappers, singers, and musicians, who, between the autumn of 2000 and the spring of 2004, took part in the projects of Theater: Playstation.

Playstation's goal was to present material drawn from actual youth culture and authentic characters as theater in an artistic (but also entertaining) form. We used interviews, improvisations, and group conversations to develop ideas and texts together. This process made very clear how significant music is as youth's means of expression.

The realization led us to develop theater in which music plays a major role—musicals, if you will, except that the aesthetic and also the music itself had to be distinct from the genre.

Our first piece, "The Dreamwanderers," concerned itself with young people's dreams, nightmares, and visions. Next, in the summer of 2002, came the music theater project "Blood on the Dance Floor," performed in a techno club, the Phonodrome on the *Reeperbahn*.

In December 2003 our musical "Die, Pop Star, Die," had its premiere at Kampnagel, Hamburg.

For me as a writer, the chance to work with young people so intensively and over such a long period of time was an extraordinary experience. (Aside from everything else, it also was great fun.) I want to thank those who, for however short or long a time, participated in Theater: Playstation. I'm especially beholden to the cast of "Die, Pop Star, Die": Lilian Arhin, Jana Behnke, Pia Hansen, Jara Jovanović, Andy Pfundstein, Mable Preach, Georg Sheljasov, Thando Walbaum, and Melanie Steffens; also, for advice and help: Susanne Schwarz, Ulrike Hilby, Felix Martin, Christian Concilio, and Lars Maué.

David Chotjewitz, Hamburg, December 2004

ABOUT THE AUTHOR

David Chotjewitz is a teacher, novelist, and playwright. His first YA novel to appear in English, *Daniel Half Human*, was a Mildred L. Batchelder Honor Book. He lives in Hamburg, Germany.

ABOUT THE TRANSLATOR

Doris Orgel has translated many Grimm tales from German and has written many books of her own in English. She lives in New York City.